Birth of a Betty

"Lucas, I have this humongous favor to ask of you. You know Sharon Clay—she's like in the midst of this major transition," I said. "I see her as a Betty-in-progress, only her ego is frantically fragile and her social skills are Jurassically grunge. What she needs is a vicious esteem builder. Something like—" I paused as though deep in thought. "Well, like showing up at a high-profile school function on the sturdy arm of a known Baldwin."

Lucas cocked his head at me. "You mean, like going to some major Alcott bender like the Monster Bash with someone like me?"

"Oh, wow! That is so brilliant. That would totally send her stock soaring," I said, then took a deep breath and went for it. "Lucas, how would you feel about taking Sharon to the Monster Bash?"

"If I didn't have a date with you?" He shut his eyes, lifted his square jaw, and gave the prospect a moment's consideration.

"You said she was a babe," I reminded him. "And, Lucas, this is so important to me."

He stood abruptly and stared down at me in disbelief. "Are you saying," he demanded, "that you want me to like blow you off and take someone else to the Bash?"

Clueless™ Books

Available from ARCHWAY Paperbacks

Cher and Cher Alike

H.B. Gilmour

AN ARCHWAY PAPERBACK
Published by POCKET BOOKS
New York London Toronto Sydney Tokyo Singapore

AN ARCHWAY PAPERBACK *Original*

An Archway Paperback published by
POCKET BOOKS, a division of Simon & Schuster Inc.
1230 Avenue of the Americas, New York, NY 10020

ISBN: 0-671-01161-8

First Archway Paperback printing July 1997

10 9 8 7 6 5 4 3

Printed in the U.S.A.

IL 7+

For my mother.

With gratitude to Trevor Johann, John Marmon, and Margaret Wolfson for their invaluable assistance. With attitude to Anne and Amira. And to Jessi, John, and Wendy, as always, with love.

Cher and Cher Alike

Chapter 1

*P*eople! People!" Poor Mr. Hall was trying to call the class to order. It was a decent yet doomed effort.

Situated on a palm-studded oasis of choice Beverly Hills real estate and surrounded by some of the world's freshest shopping venues, Bronson Alcott High School has an outstanding academic reputation.

Ten out of ten Alcott graduates go to college, most of them in chauffeured limos packed with Vuitton luggage, cutting-edge audiovisual equipment, and huge baskets of munchies from like the Gourmet Chalet in Hollywood, or mood candles, bath oils, and fragrant soaps from La Natura.

But with only ten days left before Bronson Alcott's major fall bender, the Monster Bash, the entire school was furiously immersed in party prep. In Mr. Hall's class, it was like, "Pronouns and adverbs? I don't think so."

Sitting at my desk, twirling a strand of lustrous highlighted hair around one of my excellently French-manicured fingers, I watched our teacher's futile exertion. My heart went out to the tweed-jacketed English meister. Yet even I was brutally distracted by the dance.

The Monster Bash was the premier costume op of the season, a totally chronic masquerade ball with a horror theme. There were excellent prizes for the most original getups. And although I didn't know exactly *what* I'd go as, I did have an inkling of *who* I'd go with.

Fluffy pink pen in hand, I found myself doodling the initials L.B. on the notebook page reserved for Mr. Hall's wisdom. Among the few acceptable high school boys with whom I'd even consider attending the fiesta, Lucas Burlinger, senior class hockey stud, was my number one choice.

"Who's L.B.?"

I glanced over my shoulder to find a pair of noble green eyes focused on my notebook. They belonged to the new boy at school, a dark-haired, leather-jacketed babe named Raphael, who had one fatal flaw. He was in my class. Which meant he was developmentally deprived, maturity challenged, way too young.

"Excuse me?" I said, covering the page. "It is so not something that would interest you."

"Everything about you interests me, princess," the emerald-eyed hottie asserted. "Plus, my pen just ran out of ink. Can I borrow yours?" He tilted his head and gave me this full-out Purina plea. It was a viciously effective move; he looked so puppy, all loyalty and fuzzy devotion.

So, of course I lent him my favorite feathered pen. When I tuned back in to the class discussion, the room was rampant with ensemble chat.

"Okay, let's have a show of hands." Murray, my best friend Dionne's fatal attraction, was standing at his desk surveying the class. His oversize straw golf cap sat backward on his head. The choice Phat Farm shirt he wore billowed below his knees, almost obscuring the shar-pei wrinkles of his humongous jeans. "How many Freddy Kruegers?" he asked.

Four hands went up.

"Yo, that's four for *Nightmare on Elm Street*." Murray's shadow, Sean, in a camouflage-print fishing hat, confirmed the count.

"So there'll be four Freddys at the Monster Bash." Murray jotted it down. "That's just from this class. And I got two more from algebra."

"Excuse me." My adorable friend Tai, who'd been pruning her split ends, paused to raise her cuticle scissors. "Isn't Freddy Krueger the *Halloween* psycho?" she innocently asked.

"Ouch, Tai!" Our hypercritical homey, Amber Salk, whose tangerine bouffant and faux lizard unitard so qualified her as an expert on horror, seemed shocked. "Hello, Freddy Krueger is totally *Nightmare on Elm*," she admonished. "He's got that chewed-up hat and those egregious knives for fingers."

"It's true." Mascara wand in hand, my true blue bud Dionne looked up from the magnifying mirror on her desk. "His acrylics are majorly gross. More metallic and way longer than the ones Amber was wearing last week."

Jesse Fiegenhut, the self-absorbed Adonis whose father heads a major music company, looked up from the CD collection he was cataloging. "The dude from *Halloween*—the highest grossing independent film ever," he clarified, "is Michael Myers, the mass murderer who wakes from a ten-year coma to go after Jamie Lee Curtis."

"Yo, who wouldn't?" Sean asked. "Okay, so on the real, who's going outfitted as Michael Myers?"

Tai turned to me, baffled. "Jamie Lee Curtis?" she whispered. "The Terminator's wife?"

"Yes and no, Tai," I explained as Murray and Sean resumed their apparel survey. "Jamie Lee Curtis was the babysitter in *Halloween*. And, yes, she also played Arnold Schwarzenegger's wife, only it was in *True Lies*, not *The Terminator*."

"Plus like a century ago, her mother got stabbed by Tony Curtis in *Psycho*," added the nose-ringed Olivia Ackst, whose peroxided hair sported a dark, black part.

"Not even," my friend Baez disagreed. "One—" She had just repaired a chip in her blue nail enamel so, although she was counting on her fingers, she was doing it with extreme care. "It was Tony *Perkins* who knifed Jamie Lee's mom in *Psycho*. And two, Tony *Curtis* is her father."

"And you know all this because?" Amber demanded.

"Because I am toying with going to the Monster Bash *as* Jamie Lee Curtis," Baez responded. "I thought she was brilliant as the terrorized babysitter and looked frantically awesome in that slinky polyester shirt and those hip-hugger jeans."

Kimberly Woo, whose glossy black locks, unsheared practically from birth, cascaded down her back and fanned out on her seat, observed, "I'm a solid Jamie Lee fan, but her hair's so short. Probably I'll do Elvira."

"Okay, so we've got one Elvira. And that's six Michael Myerses, right?" Murray sucked his lip in concentration. "Okay, now, who's thinking R.L. Stine? You know, bloodsucking gnomes, face-eating masks."

Out of the corner of my eye, I saw Mr. Hall rubbing his head in exasperation. The sparse curls that bordered his bald spot were in disarray. I felt his pain.

I tried to catch Dionne's eye. Beyond the clean coincidence that we are both named for pop idols of our parents' generation, De and I are bonded in many ways. We are blessed with slammin' genes, rampant popularity, raging fashion sense, and of course, the Gold cards to actualize it. Monster role models for the femme end of our class, we also share a frantic zest for life and irrepressible leadership abilities. At the moment, however, we were so not in synch.

Dionne was engrossed in cosmetic betterment. I was experiencing Mr. Hall's anguish. I knew I had to act, with or without my t.b.'s support.

"Hello! Excuse me!" I stood up. "Everyone, I think Mr. Hall has something he'd like to say."

"Is it about the Monster Bash?" Sean demanded.

"Actually, in a way it is," Mr. Hall announced, much to everyone's surprise. His small but furiously intelligent-looking eyes were suddenly alight with inspiration. "I haven't seen this level of enthusiasm since I canceled last week's quiz," he continued. "So let's capitalize on class enthusiasm with a book report—"

He didn't even get a chance to finish his sentence before the groaning and grumbling began.

"Hey, yo, everyone!" Suddenly Raphael was on his feet. "You heard what Cher said," he called, hiking up the supple collar of his sleek leather jacket. "So let's listen up, okay? Cut the old guy some slack." Then the ragin' recent addition gave me this golden smile and sat down again, oblivious to the hoots and hisses he'd unleashed.

Mr. Hall cleared his throat. "Yes, well, thank you,

Raphael," he said. "Your assignment, due two weeks from today, class, is to read and write a report on a literary horror classic." Then with this pleased little smile, he addressed us again. "I think that most of you will be surprised at how many riveting works of fiction there are to choose from."

He went on in that vein for a while. The whole class was like quiet and nodding politely. But gradually everyone started drifting back to more stimulating activities. For Amber, Tai, and Baez, this involved various self-improvement procedures. For me it meant cellularly speed-dialing Dionne, who had completed her experiment with forest green mascara and was now trying on earrings two rows and three seats away.

My best bud picked up on the first ring. "'Zup, girlfriend?" she said without even waiting to hear my voice.

"Dionne, since when do you answer your phone that way?" I asked. "I mean, like what if it wasn't me calling? What if it was Mr. Lehman?"

"Duh, then I guess my caller ID would have listed Mr. Lehman's number instead of yours. And, right, like I'd really give Bronson Alcott's too harsh principal my unlisted cell phone digits."

I smacked my forehead but lightly. "Caller ID. Of course, De. I forgot. Angst can so curdle the brain."

"Angst? Excuse me, Cher, but angst and you are bitterly incompatible."

"Were," I corrected my foremost friend. "The Monster Bash is ten days away, and has you-know-who even heard from you-know-hunk about going?"

"If Lucas Burlinger is the Baldwin in question, live angst free, girlfriend," De said supportively. "There is no one else in the entire Beverly Hills school and shopping district that he would even think about asking to the Bash. Except maybe me," she teased, "if Murray and I were not such a chronic match. And speaking of my man, is he conversationally available?"

"Then you and your boo have settled your trust issue?" I asked.

A mere two hours earlier, in the school parking lot, De and Murray's verbal sparring had drawn a decent crowd. From what I'd gathered, over the heads of those who'd arrived early and drawn ringside positions, Murray was wearing a new aftershave. He claimed that a sample of the cologne had been thrust into his hand as he'd innocently browsed Hugo Boss shirts in the men's department at Neiman's. De wasn't buying the tale. She felt there was something more significant and sinister about the scent switch.

Just who was he trying to impress? she'd demanded. And then she'd gone into this impressive rave about smell and how no sense reaches more deeply into our emotional center. Murray countered—very effectively, I thought—with a discussion on trust as a vital ingredient in any human relationship.

"He promised to show me the sample vial after school, and I promised to have total faith in his fidelity," my best bud now said. "And to not challenge his devotion for two whole weeks. So we agreed to a moratorium on public debates until after the dance. Is he handy?"

I craned my neck in Murray's direction. He was leaning way over into the aisle. Two desks away, Sean was similarly bent. I heard the telltale whine of a tiny motor. "Toyz 'N the Hood are drag racing their remote control vehicles," I informed De. "But hold on. I'll see if Murray will take a call."

Just then the door opened and Sharon Clay, grunge goddess, slunk into the room, hugging her books to her chest.

"Speaking of horror classics," Amber blurted, eyeing the girl with curdling disapproval.

"Amber," I said, passing her my cellular, "if you can resign your Supreme Court duties for a moment, tell Murray that De is on the line."

"Hello, I was not judging," Amber insisted, casting a withering look my way. "It's a full-out fact that Sharon's fashion choices display a brutal disregard for community standards."

I hated to admit it, but Sergeant Salk of the couture patrol was not entirely wrong. I studied our tardy classmate as Amber passed my cell phone to Murray. In terms of garb, the girl did seem to be sinking in sartorial quicksand.

The strap of Sharon's faded pink slip dress drooped over one of her rounded shoulders. The black thigh-highs she wore with scuffed urban combat boots were brutally vintage. And the straw-textured hair she regularly flung back from her forehead embraced the entire blond spectrum, from Heather Locklear to Dennis Rodman. Plus she was sporting a safety pin through her left eyebrow, which was such an accessory blunder.

With a subdued wave to her best friend, Olivia, whose nose ring, I now noted, was heinously tarnished, Sharon headed directly for Mr. Hall. "I'm sorry I'm late," she murmured, handing him her excuse slip. "Really, I'm like consumed with regret."

I found myself unexpectedly moved by the girl's garmental cluelessness and aura of schleppy defeat. In Sharon's favor, however, if you could get past the obvious fashion faux pas, she had a Kate Moss bod and basically decent features. Plus a proper conditioning mousse could probably salvage her scalp before the hair police busted her for follicle abuse.

A hand tapped my shoulder and broke my concentration. It was Raphael again.

"So like do you have a favorite?" he asked, tucking a lock of thick black hair back behind his ear.

"A favorite what?" I asked as the bell rang. I stood up and signaled Murray to return my cell phone.

Raphael stood, too, towering over me. "Author," he explained. "Like whose classic horror novel are you going to do your report on?"

I found the combination of his outstanding looks and the rampant devotion with which his green eyes scanned my face way hypnotic. "I haven't really thought it through yet," I confessed. "I'm torn between Stephen King and V.C. Andrews. Of course King would be the popular choice," I added, glancing at Murray, who held up his hand to assure me he was concluding his cellular schmooze.

"I already threw you a kiss," I heard him grumbling to De. "What you think I was doing, sucking food outta my teeth? If you had kisser ID instead of caller ID, you wouldn't be doggin' me now." Mashing down his straw cap in rampant frustration, Murray clicked off and tossed me my Motorola.

Raphael's leather-clad arm shot out and intercepted it. "So, if most of the class goes with King, then you'll take the V.C. path, right?" he said, handing me the phone. He walked with me to the door. "'Cause that's who you are, princess—an individualist, a rebel, a true original."

"That is so astute," I responded, conscious of his fierce yet adoring gaze. "I mean, for someone who just met me last week."

"I've known you all my life," the boy insisted, stopping suddenly and blocking the exit. "Because you're just like me. We're two of a kind, Cher."

"Not even!" Sharon was suddenly part of the conversation. "I'm sorry," she blurted out, going all blotchy with embarrassment. "I just mean, er, that is so not possible."

"Excuse me?" I said, amazed at her passionate intrusion. Raphael glanced at her, too, and Sharon immediately dropped her head to avoid his gaze.

"Because there is totally nobody like you, Cher," she mumbled into the books she was hugging.

Sharon's tawdry comrade, Olivia, was leaving the classroom and overheard the remark. She rolled her eyes and stuck her index finger into her mouth, miming nausea.

To her credit, Sharon narrowed her eyes dismissively at the girl.

"Often imitated never duplicated, that's my homey," Dionne quipped mischeviously, scrunching past us into the hallway. "Algebra calls. Kiss, kiss, girlfriend. I'm bailing. Beep me after school," she added, waiting for Murray to join her.

In deep discussion, he and Sean moved through the door. Their XL baggies dragged along the floor, sweeping a path through fallen lipstick tubes, CD-player batteries, and crumpled Amex receipts. "I know I said 'Tales from the 'Hood' was a fly suggestion. I'm just rethinking our outfit options, that's all," Murray was saying. "Right now I'm leaning toward a more ethnic Afro roots kind of thing."

"Word up." Sean was psyched. "I can totally relate. How 'bout we go with urban vampire attire, you know, like these bad black satin capes, only all messed up and scary like the Cryptkeeper meets Blacula."

"Naw, bro." Murray wrinkled his nose, pleating the lip fuzz he tried to pass off as a mustache. "If we gonna house the competition, we got to represent."

"I recognize," Sean agreed. "I'm for snaggin' first prize."

"Excuse me, Cher," Sharon said as we followed the great costume debate out into the corridor. "I mean, I'm sorry. But like do you think I could talk to you? Alone?" she mumbled, glancing at Raphael, who was at my side.

Raphael looked from me to her. Under his scrutiny, Sharon's blotches bloomed again.

"It's brutally urgent," she added.

"Will you excuse us, please?" I asked Raphael.

He nodded, hiked up his collar again, and said, "For you, anything." Then he disappeared into the busy corridor, leaving the rich scent of Prada leather in his wake.

"I couldn't help but notice your eyebrow." I turned my attention to Sharon. "It looks way irritated. You might try swabbing it with polysporin ointment when you get home. As a temporary measure, I may have some Vitamin E capsules in my backpack."

Sharon touched the little safety pin over her eye and kind of winced. "I should have sterilized it," she confessed, "only I was already late to class and I just grabbed the first pin I saw and, you know, stuck it in."

"Time management is a harsh master," I responded sympathetically. "Still, one should never allow oneself to be rushed into making poor—or painful—accessory choices."

But Sharon's focus had strayed. I followed her gaze and saw Lucas emerging through the shuffling ranks of students moving toward their next class.

Raphael was all East Coast pale, a dreamy Johnny Depp with excellently styled dark locks. But Lucas, in his clean J. Crew togs, sun-bleached hair, and surfer's tan, was like the total preppie poster boy for California Dreamin', a golden Chris O'Donnell riding a rugged Keanu edge.

"Cher, this is so choice," Lucas called, bounding toward me. "I mean, I was just thinking of you. I've been meaning to catch up with you and like, you know, ask you if you want to—"

"Oh, I am so sorry." Sharon cut him off. "How bitterly bad is my timing? I'm way contrite."

"Am I interrupting you guys or something?" Lucas looked from Sharon to me. His azure eyes blinked apologetically. "I can catch you later, Cher. Actually, I'm like late for team pictures anyway." Before I could reply, he flashed me a heart-melting grin, gave this quick wave, and jogged down the corridor toward the doors leading to the sports complex.

I couldn't believe what had just happened. For one brief moment I'd stood at the threshold of fiesta fulfillment, then fate had slammed the door in my face. He was going to ask me to the dance, my mind whimpered. I tried to keep my expression friendly and my smile from wavering as I turned back to Sharon.

"Lucas reigns, doesn't he?" she said, pulling up her slip strap.

"Brutally," I agreed.

Suddenly, Raphael was back. "Princess, I almost forgot," he said, waving my fluffy pink pen at me. "This is yours, isn't it?"

"Well, let's see," I replied. "It's got my initials on it. And I lent it to you less than twenty minutes ago. So, duh, I guess so."

The Depp-esque hottie grinned. "What a babe. Hey, thanks."

"De nada," I assured him, taking the pen. "Would you excuse us please, Raphael? Sharon and I have something urgent to discuss."

"Right." He stared at me with this dark intensity. "You're the best," he said, then bailed.

"I'm sorry for all the interruptions," I told Sharon.

"Oh, that's okay. I mean, you're frantically popular so I totally understand. Anyway, it was nothing. Like, you know, no big deal." So said the girl's quivering lips, but her eyes were rampant with tear potential. She was clearly in a raw emotional state. Or maybe it was just safety pin distress. "Just like totally forget about it," she insisted, backing away.

"Sharon, wait," I called, reaching out to her. "Remember, a problem shared is a problem halved."

"You are so perfect," she replied with this perplexing hint of sarcasm. And then, hunched over her books, multiblond hair crackling, she turned on her stack-heeled combat boots and fled, leaving me to puzzle over what her problem was and, worse, still Baldwin-less for the Bash.

Chapter 2

*E*mpty calories are an ugly option," Dionne's voice warned me from the speakerphone in my kitchen.

It was four o'clock. I was staring into the freezer compartment of our refrigerator. Lucas had not contacted me since the afternoon's corridor debacle. The ice cream bars in our fridge had begun singing to me.

"Read the label, Cher," De urged, trying to help me avoid a tragic gorge. "Start with the calories, then go to sugar content and grams of saturated fat."

"But they're covered in thick bittersweet chocolate, De, which is so gourmet. They're way too rich to be classified as junk food. I mean, isn't chocolate found in nature?"

"Not even!" De tried to snap me back to reality. "I hate to do this to you, girlfriend, but visualize the midriff bulge of ice cream bloat destroying the delicate lines of that Anna Sui pink and gold lace crop top you just bought."

I shuddered, slammed shut the freezer door, and turned my back on temptation.

I have to say that the sight of our kitchen helped restore my self-esteem. I had recently worked with a renowned decorator to have the room renovated. Daddy had balked at the bills, but ultimately he'd signed Hervé's invoices. Gone were the pastel appliances of my youth. The galley now gleamed with chic industrial steel.

"Dionne, you are truly my best and most supportive bud," I called toward the phone. "So, you were saying?"

"Oh, about Murray? He's like all into how I don't trust him. Which is so not true," De replied, emphatically. "Only I caught him coming out of the *library!*"

There was a silver Jensen fruit bowl on the new stainless-steel counter. From it I selected a ripe mango and carried it over to our new aluminum worktable. "And?" I prodded Dionne.

"And, duh, the last time you saw Murray enter a library was when?"

"Like never," I said, beginning the arduous but satisfying mango-peeling process. "But I find it fiercely commendable."

"Yes, and so, I'm sure, does Bronson Alcott's new librarian, the West Coast winner of the Jada Pinkett look-alike contest! Have you seen her yet?"

"Miss Brittany? A brutal babe," I agreed. "And so young for a career in books. I mean, she looks barely out of her teens."

"As if!" De disagreed. "She is so over twenty. Kimberly guessed like twenty-two."

"Not even! You think she's had collagen work?"

"Ask Murray." De cut me short. "He's the one who lingered at the library, doing—and I quote—'research.'"

"I thought you were turning over a new leaf, girl-friend. You vowed to trust the boy," I pointed out. "Speaking of research, are you still thinking Stephen King? I mean, are you going with like *Carrie* or *Cujo* for Mr. Hall's class?"

I carried the mango peels across the room, dropped them into the sink, and turned on the disposal unit. "I'm leaning in the V.C. direction," I called over the hum of the mechanical mulcher.

"Who are you shouting at?" The question was posed by a too familiar masculine voice. I spun toward the door and my fears were confirmed. Josh, my hopelessly PC stepbrother, had left the cheerless laundry hamper of a dorm room he called home to invade our comfy casa again. And seeing no one in the kitchen with me, he obviously thought I'd wigged.

"Nice," Josh mused, taking in the new decor. "Very twenty-first century. Right out of *House & Garden's* special sci-fi issue."

Josh came to us as part of a package deal. He is my father's most recent ex-wife's son by a former marriage. So, although he calls himself my brother and still thinks of Daddy as his father, he is not of our blood.

"I so appreciate your style sense, Josh," I greeted my non-kin. "Tell me more about the bargains at T.J. Maxx."

"What are you doing home?" he replied. "The malls don't close for hours."

"I happen to be talking about books with Dionne," I informed him, pointing to the wall phone.

"Oh, is that Josh? Hi, Josh," De called to him. She has always thought the boy was a full-out Baldwin. Which, strictly in the looks division, he may be, but he is way lacking in the killer charisma of the brothers Alec, Billy, and Daniel.

"Hi, Dionne," Josh called over his shoulder as he began inspecting the contents of our cupboards. Then he glanced at me with this annoying smirk. "Please, don't let me interrupt your literary discussion. I'm just hunting up snacks. I've been helping Dad go over some depositions."

"That's Dad, as in *my* dad, correct?"

Josh gave me one of his long-suffering looks. "Yes, that would be Dad, as in your dad, my stepdad, Mel Horowitz, attorney at law, litigator to the stars, the pit bull of the appellate court. He who has requested nourishment. I'm just pulling together a snack for us." Then he added with a mocking grin, "Of course, I wouldn't have to if Lucy was here. But I understand you're enriching her life again."

"I am not enriching Lucy's life," I corrected him. "I am improving my father's chances at longevity. If our housekeeper doesn't learn the secrets of low-fat cuisine, it's pacemaker city for Daddy. And anyway, the 'Wonderful World of Tofu' is an excellent seminar. I'm sure Lucy will get a lot out of it."

"Cher, want me to check back later?" Dionne's voice called from the speakerphone.

"No." I whacked at the skinned mango. "Let's take Josh's personality into consideration and pretend we're alone. So what made you decide to go the Stephen King route?"

"Okay," said De, "two things. Like one, you can get

most of his books on audio, videocassette, and probably CD-ROM. And two, because he is, after all, the master of the horror genre, an excellent storyteller who, I personally think, leaves all his rivals eating dirt in the dust. Except V.C. Andrews, of course."

"I have tremendous respect for Stephen King, De," I conceded, arranging healthful mango slices in a circular pattern on my plate. "But face it, everyone who isn't all R.L. Stine, R.L. Stine, R.L. Stine, is all Stephen King, Stephen King, Stephen King. I mean, when it comes to horror classics, like who does that leave besides V.C.?"

A snort of amusement greeted this question. It came from the cabinet area behind me, where Josh was foraging.

"Excuse me, Dionne," I announced loudly. "It seems that our conversation has taken the place of the lame espresso house poetry, girls in Birkenstocks, and 'Nick at Night' reruns that Josh usually finds so entertaining."

"I'm sorry," the step-sib responded, "but it's ridiculous to talk about horror classics and not even mention Edgar Allan Poe or Bram Stoker's *Dracula* or Mary Shelley's *Frankenstein*."

"Like hello," I begged to differ. "We're supposed to do book reports, Josh, not anthropology. Those volumes are so geriatric."

"Were they even written in this decade?" De chimed in on the speakerphone.

"The books may be old, but the authors weren't," Josh persisted, "at least, in the case of *Frankenstein*."

"Thank you, your Smartness." It was my turn to scoff. "I'm sure the guys who wrote those oldies but ghoulies were mere teens, right?"

"Actually, Mary Shelley was," Josh said, without turning from his task, which apparently was to empty the entire munchie section of our pantry into convenient portable bowls. I was appalled at the tawdry heap of treats he'd plucked from our once abundantly stocked shelves—a two-pound bag of barbecue potato chips that I'd never seen before, a box of chocolate-covered peanuts that would feed a viewing group of four at the Fox Village cinema in Westwood, and a festive holiday tin of cheddar-flavored popcorn.

"You call that parade of saturated fats a snack?" I challenged. "That is not food, Josh. Food nurtures. What you have in front of you is cholesterol in crunch form. Don't even think about foisting that heart-attack fest on Daddy."

"Mary Shelley was what?" De made the mistake of asking. "Josh, what were you saying?"

"She was nineteen," he called to her, "when she wrote one of the greatest ghost stories of all time."

I popped a juicy chunk of mango into my mouth, perched on one of our new Deco stools, and, chin in hand, prepared myself for the literary cryptkeeper's lecture. Which, I have to say, turned out to be not just unexpectedly fascinating, but majorly fresh. Because Mary Shelley and I had so much in common!

First, the author of *Frankenstein* was a woman, which I could immediately relate to. And according to Josh, she'd begun the book when she was this golden, headstrong adolescent just like me.

Also her mom, a spirited and renowned feminist, died when Mary was born, so she was reared by her esteemed philosopher dad. And of course my mom, one of the awesome Bettys of her day, whose interests ranged from designer disco wear to serious do-gooding, died when I was infantile, as well. And my father is this extremely prominent person who can wax way philosophical, especially on the subject of greens fees at the Hillcrest Country Club.

But best of all, Mary Shelley was an actual Uma; a brutally popular babe with like this immense Alanis Morissette–type brain who hung with the foremost poet Baldwins of her day, Lord Byron and Percy Shelley.

"They were stuck in this villa in Switzerland," Josh told us, "the rebellious young poets, Byron and Shelley, and Mary and her half-sister, Jane. It had been raining for days. They were bored. To amuse themselves, they started reading these ancient German ghost tales they'd found in the villa. And one night Lord Byron suggested that they try writing ghost stories of their own."

"And did they?" De prompted as Josh opened the burnished double doors of the fridge.

"At ease. I'm just looking for milk," he informed me.

"Well, you won't find it in the ice cream compartment," I remarked. "And anyway, Daddy's only allowed skim."

Before the faux-bro could protest, my Motorola went off. I clicked it on. "Cher, hey, it's me." Covering the mouthpiece, I rasped into the speakerphone, "De, it's Lucas. I'm history, girlfriend. Back in five!" I punched off speakerphone and went cellular. "Hi, Lucas. So how did the team photos turn out?"

"They won't be ready till next week," he replied. "I'm probably going to be July."

"I don't think I understand," I said, confused.

"Well, June or July, the guy said. We're doing this Hockey Hunks calendar, you know, as a school fundraiser. And this guy who was like art-directing the thing said I was definitely early summer. You wouldn't think being a hunk was hard work, right? But the shoot took hours."

Across the room I saw Josh leaving the kitchen, looking suspiciously sheepish. "Where are you now?" I asked Lucas.

"I'm still at the sports center. Only now I'm at hockey practice. We just took a break and I thought, hey, this is as good a time as any, right?"

I tossed back my golden hair and tried to contain my glee. "As good a time as any . . . for what?" I asked in this cheerful, innocent way.

"Hey, hey, hey. Don't do that," Lucas said with sudden upset.

"Excuse me?" I was way perplexed by his mood swing.

"Not you, Cher," he assured me. "Hey, stop. Nothing's that bad."

"Lucas? What's wrong? Who are you talking to?" I asked.

"Listen, Cher, there's someone here that like needs my help. I'll call you back. Or else I'll catch you tomorrow, okay? Jeez, take it easy, would you?" And he was gone, his honeyed voice replaced by a mocking dial tone.

I stared at the receiver in disbelief, then clicked off. The blinding metallic glare of kitchen appliances did nothing to soothe me. Had I made a major mistake? Not about Lucas. I knew there had to be a sensible explanation for his whack behavior. It was the renovation I had begun to doubt. Suddenly, I missed the syrupy solace of petal pink and key lime equipment, the warm wood tones and whimsical Italian tiles of my youth.

Downing the last mango slice, I left the shining cold steel of our new kitchen and headed toward the sounds of warm laughter coming from the study.

In the entry hall outside Daddy's den, I paused to stare up at the portrait of Mom. She died when I was practically new, but I like to believe she's keeping an eye on me. No matter how I'm feeling, it always cheers me to look at her fab face.

I never burden Mom with my problems. So, even though I was a tad bummed, I gave her this little wave and put a positive spin on the day's events. "My life is totally golden, Ma," I assured her. "I mean, I'm probably definitely going to the dance with Bronson Alcott's July calendar boy. Plus, Josh just told me about this inspiring little horror tale I might do my book report on. And, Ma, the mother of the author was a bitterly benevolent Betty just like you. Neat, huh?"

The sound of my voice, however soft, seemed to unleash this flurry of activity inside Daddy's study. "Put it away. Hurry up," I heard. Papers rustled, file folders fell, a drawer slammed. Then Josh and Daddy started laughing again. Only not quite aloud. It was more like this hushed, bad-boy snicker, something between a cackle and a cough.

When I peeked inside, Josh was all hunched over a pile of depositions and Daddy gave me this guilty little wave. "Hi, honey," he said. "We're very busy. Boy, have we been working hard. Right, Josh? This case is a real backbreaker."

"You know, Daddy, among the items from the garbage food group that Dr. Jacobs says you should avoid," I reminded him, "ice cream is way up on the list."

"Ice cream?" He seemed hurt by the accusation.

"Duh. There's a telltale ring of chocolate around your lips thick enough to feed Somalia, Daddy. Plus that creamy substance dripping from the file drawer onto your sporty new Cole Haan loafers looks suspiciously like a melting Dove bar. Unless, of course, there's a nervous pigeon in your desk."

I left the boys going, "um, er, uh," and climbed the sweeping marble staircase to my room where, at any moment, I was sort of sure, Lucas would phone and finally ask me to the dance.

Chapter 3

So you're over V.C.?" Dionne asked me the next morning. We were breakfasting on cappuccino and croissants at our reserved table in the Quad.

"My bogus bro can be a major pain, but I'm extremely psyched about Mary Shelley," I confirmed. "I'm definitely thinking of doing my report on *Frankenstein.*"

"I've been rethinking, as well," De confessed, stirring her decaf capp. "You were so right. Everyone is reading Stephen King. And how bad can *Frankenstein* be if an elderly hottie like Robert De Niro was in the movie?"

It was a brilliant morning. The patio of the school cafeteria was awash with light. Sunshine filtered through layers of smog. You could just tell the sky above the haze was probably a sparkling, cloudless blue.

De lifted her Cazale sunglasses and examined the rich Italian brew before her. "So, Lucas never called back?" she asked, spooning cinnamon specks out of the foam.

I brushed a croissant flake off the lap of my little lace dress by Helmut Lang. "Not last night," I confirmed. "De, didn't you tell Miles, the beverage boy, that you didn't want condiments in your coffee?"

"We've been coming here for ages. You'd think he'd know by now," she said. "So, who do you think he was talking to?"

"Miles?" I asked.

De paused, a spoonful of cinnamon-bearing foam poised above her cup. "Really?" She seemed viciously baffled. "What makes you think Lucas was talking to Miles last night?"

"Let's start over," I suggested. "I have no idea who the troubled person was. But someone was so excessively distressed that my compassionate Baldwin had to tear himself from our conversation to perform instant disaster relief. I guess when I catch up with Lucas later today, I'll get the whole story."

"You could do that." Amber slid onto the bench across from me. Her 'do du jour, two high-flying ponytails that sat like floppy horns on either side of her head, waggled and jiggled as she settled in. "Or," she said, grinning smugly, "I could solve that mystery for you."

"I choose door number two," De said. "Dish, girl."

"Do you even know what we're talking about?" I challenged. Amber stared over the skinny tortoiseshell rims of her Giorgio sunshades at me. "Oh, no. Not unless it's who distracted luscious Lucas Burlinger while he was on the phone by crying her heavily penciled eyes out at the sports complex late yesterday afternoon while I was composing a hockey cheer."

"You were there?" I marveled.

"I viciously voyeured everything!"

"Talk to us, girlfriend," De demanded.

"Okay, well, as I said"—Amber leaned forward, every fiber of her being poised to tell all—"I was working with the pep squad. And I was arduously creating this amazing hockey cheer. You know, like 'We've got the players, we've got the pucks, we've got the parents with the choicest investment porfolios!'"

Amber paused, waiting for us to acknowledge her genius.

"It doesn't rhyme," De said.

"I know." Amber shrugged. "I was going to go, 'We've got the players, we've got the pucks, we've got the parents who earn big bucks,' but it just sounded crass."

"Amber, you're a totally major talent," I said, eager to get the girl back on track. "So after you composed that def motivational anthem, you saw who crying?"

"Sharon Clay, the lingerie-for-streetwear queen. You can imagine my surprise. I mean, who expects tears from a girl who can safety pin her lids?"

Amber pointed at my croissant, and I pushed it toward her. "Sharon was bitterly distraught," she continued. Tearing my breakfast pastry in two, she began wolfing down her half. "The girl was actually crying so copiously that not only was her so not waterproof midnight blue mascara viciously streaking her face, but I feared she'd actually rust her eyebrow clip and require like a tetanus shot."

"And Lucas viewed this scene?" I asked.

"He could so not have avoided it." Amber blotted her lips with De's napkin and nodded. The tattered red banners of her ponytails bobbed emphatically. "Sharon was unabashedly in his face. And when the Baldwin clicked off his cellular and turned his attention to her, guess whose name came blubbering to the surface of her swampy conversation?"

"You can have the rest of the croissant," I said.

"Do the initials *C.H.* ring a bell?" Amber asked archly, pulling my plate across the table.

"Duh. Let's see?" Dionne's annoyance was barely restrained. She tilted her head thoughtfully at the hockey bard. "Is it Courtney Love? No, that's an L. Is it Sheryl Crow? Whoops, that's *S.C.* Oh. Could it be Cher Horowitz?"

"You don't have to go postal, De," Amber admonished. "Yes. It was Cher. Sharon was grilling Lucas about—and this is her, not me, so please don't get all bent, okay?—about what he sees in Cher."

"She was asking my honey what he sees in me?" I queried.

"Yes. And this you will totally not believe. It seems that grunge girl has a crush on a guy who thinks Cher's chronic."

"Well, that could be anyone with eyes," my loyal bud, Dionne, reminded her. "Case in point," she added, grinning suddenly. "Here comes noble new boy bearing gift."

Amber and I turned to see Raphael heading for our table. The tall, dark-haired hottie was practically hidden by the enormous gift-wrapped package he was carrying.

"Princess," he said, plopping the beribboned box down on our table and sliding onto the bench next to me. He took my hand and pressed it to his chest. "Did you ever feel anything like that?" he asked.

"Of course I have," I responded, withdrawing my digits. "I have tons of leather goods from Prada and other important style emporiums."

He gave me one of his intense green-eyed gazes. "It's

not about apparel, princess. It's about my heart. Feel how it's beating?"

"You must be viciously out of shape," Amber commented. "I mean, how heavy could that package be?"

"I'm not fibrillating because of flab," Raphael responded. "It's you, Cher, that makes my heart twitch uncontrollably. Open your gift. I think you're really going to like it."

De and Amber watched as I tore off the wrapping and pulled open the carton. There before me, in alphabetical order, were the complete works of V.C. Andrews.

"Raphael," I began, not actually speechless but kind of at a loss. Which is so not me. Basically, I'm way verbal and usually get by with only minor mind-to-mouth filtering. But here were these expectant eyes cruising my face and a grin anticipating gratitude already dimpling the boy's strong jaws. "What a surprise," I managed to continue. "It's a book fair in a box!"

"But we are so over V.C. Andrews—and even Stephen King," De intervened, shooting straight from her Dolce & Gabbana–draped hip. "It's sad but true, Raphael. Cher and I have moved on to Mary Shelley's chronic horror tale, which was highly recommended by a knowledgeable college-type person."

Raphael's smile turned ironic. "I get it," he said, with a trace of bitterness. "I'm thinking *Flowers in the Attic*, and you're into *Frankenstein*. You must think I'm so shallow."

"*Flowers in the Attic* busts fresh." As they approached our table, Murray and Sean caught the tail end of Raph's remarks. "V.C. Andrews is my idol," Sean continued.

"For an Anglo-American experience in terror, maybe. But when it comes to killer chillers, Afrocentric tales like

'The Hairy Man' and 'Ananta the Spider' are butter to the mutha," Murray announced.

"Funky, fresh, and fly," Sean agreed. He was sporting a new, knee-length Lakers jacket and a fuzzy, baby blue ski cap with the price tag still hanging from it.

" 'The Hairy Man'? Did we see that?" De asked me. "Who was in it?"

I shrugged. "Gibby Haynes of the Surfers?" It was a wild guess. "Outstanding chapeau," I told Sean as he began pawing through the book box. "It would look especially awesome on me. That shade so accents my own eye color, which is slightly more cerulean, or sky blue."

Sean bobbed his head. "Thank you," he said, then stretched out his arms and spun slowly, showing off the jacket.

"You like those threads?" Raphael asked me.

"Hip-hop is a valid fashion alternative and, yes, I think Sean's dual sports theme demonstrates outstanding flair. Especially that wicked ski bonnet. But, Raphael," I added, touching his leather-sheathed arm, "I just want to say that your gift was viciously thoughtful. And I would never call you shallow."

"Nothing wrong with shallow." Murray went into male bonding mode. "It's a viable macho position."

"Word up," Sean agreed. "Say it loud, I'm shallow and I'm proud!" Then he slapped hands and knocked knuckles with Murray, and the two of them started cackling hysterically.

Dionne rolled her eyes at them. "It's Boyz 2 Infantz," she said. "Just ignore them, like the brain fairy did."

"Now I'm never giving you my hat," Sean said. And he and Murray started laughing and slapping hands all over again.

"How about giving it to me?" Raphael asked. "I mean, since Cher doesn't want the books and you're a big-time Andrews fan—"

"You talking about a trade?" Sean was suddenly all business. "Is that what you're saying? Like my fly hat in exchange for the entire V.C. oeuvre? Every book my main man ever wrote? Including the classic chiller *Flowers in the Attic?*"

"And *Petals on the Wind* and *If There Be Thorns,* and so much more." Raphael nodded.

Sean's dark eyes narrowed in concentration. You could practically hear his rusty thinking mechanism cranking out a decision. Suddenly, his pursed lips stretched into this sly grin. "Done." He removed his hat and handed it to Raphael, who, in turn, presented the adorable head warmer to me.

"Enjoy," the boy said, bringing my hand to his lips and planting a kiss on my knuckles. "Got a date with chemistry in five. Catch you later, princess."

"That was a furiously gallant gesture," De said as Raphael slipped off into the stream of students heading for class.

"Sucker," Sean called after him, digging through his newly acquired book cache. "V.C. be my man." Triumphantly, he waved a copy of *Flowers* at us. "This guy writes so fine, you be needing an emergency goose-bumpectomy by page two."

"V.C. Andrews is a woman," Murray said.

"Naw. Not even!" Sean went into vicious denial. "I mean, here, look at this. You don't see no woman writing this stuff." He started flipping through the pages of *Flowers in the Attic.* "This is chill city. Fiction so fine it makes you hold your breath till you go bluer than my formerly favorite cap." Suddenly, Sean's jaw slackened. "Hello. Uh-oh. Wassup with this?" he gasped, staring at the opened book.

Murray snatched and studied it. "It's a library book," he reported. "Says right here, 'Property of Santa Monica Public Library.'"

Sean opened another volume. "This one, too," he murmured, showing De and me the stamped notice on the inside flap of the book.

"This one's from Glendale Public," I said, paging through *Seeds of Yesterday*.

Amber was digging into the pile now. "They've all been lifted from libraries." She was outraged. "Public libraries. Which means that our parents, whatever their tax avoidance status, be it arcane shelters or forward-looking retirement funds, have like actually paid for these books!"

De was more direct. "Tscha, Sean, you got brutally played!" she said.

But everyone else turned to me.

Which was no great surprise or anything. Both Dionne and I are furiously attuned to being sought-after style setters. Our peers constantly solicit our opinions, compliment our taste, and check our reactions. So the sensation of eyes anxiously boring into me was way familiar.

"What you going to do?" Sean challenged, turning to look with longing at the hat, which was sitting in the center of our table.

I thought it over, weighing the pros and cons. The ski cap's color was a definite plus. But I had at least three other hats in similar shades. And what was important to me? Fuzzy headgear from the fashion pages of *Vibe* with a double-digit price tag hanging off it or the feelings of my homeys, even if they were literary chauvinists. The pain in Sean's eyes answered my question.

"I'll probably never wear it," I confessed. "And if I did I'd definitely cut off that tag."

"You'd brutally disfigure my lid?" He was miserable.

"So why don't you take it back," I continued.

"Word up!" Murray demonstrated his approval with a glittering dental display.

"What about the books?" Amber demanded.

"We can leave them on the steps of the library," De responded, Solomon-like. "They'll know how to take care of them."

"I don't understand how Raphael could have done such a thing," Amber said.

"Be generous, Amber," I urged. "I know what he did was wrong. I am so not in favor of snagging public property. Still, I think I understand."

De nodded and totally spoke for me when she said, "Larceny in the name of love is no crime. Anyone can see how the boy feels about Cher."

Chapter 4

*U*nfortunately, anyone included Lucas. How was I to know that my hockey honey had been downing a healthful juice nearby? And that he'd witnessed Raphael's brash kiss.

Murray and Sean had ambled off to class. De, Amber, and I were getting ready to do the same, just strapping on our stuffed animal backpacks, when Lucas appeared.

"Hey, Cher, wait up," the blazingly fine senior said, sauntering up to our table. "Got a minute?" The boy was dazzling, all sculpted 'ceps and pecs and lats and abs rippling through his gold-and-chocolate cotton cardigan.

"Sure," I said, saluting him with a furiously fond smile.

"For you," De announced helpfully, "she'd blow off algebra *and* P.E."

"What is that supposed to be, a sacrifice?" Amber snorted tartly. "I'd skip out on them for nothing."

"Come on, girlfriend." De grabbed Amber's arm. "We've got to bail," she called. "Have fun, you two."

Lucas picked up one of the textbooks I hadn't had time to toss into my pack yet. He started leafing through it as we walked. I think it was my algebra book. He wasn't actually reading it, just looking at the pictures— or x's and y's. Whatever.

It was such a boy thing to do, one of those fully transparent, fidgety male diversion ploys. He was so adorable. "Sorry about last night," he began, blue eyes fastened on some random equation.

We were ambling across campus, and every few feet our fellow students would wave or smile or shout out a greeting. Lucas hardly noticed the attention we were drawing. But I always feel obliged to acknowledge it.

"I know all about what happened," I confessed, waggling my digits at an ardent fan. "And I want you to know, Lucas, that I am so proud of you. Helping others is totally my credo."

"Really?" He didn't quite slam shut the book, but he did give me a full frontal gaze.

"Absolutely. De and I average two point three make-overs a semester. Desperate girls are always after us for dating advice, shopping tips, nutrition pointers—"

"But how do you know what happened last night?" the confused athlete asked.

"Amber was at the rink, composing a cheer," I explained. "She caught the entire heart-wrenching scene. I think it was way noble of you to offer poor Sharon solace, although I have to say, last night I was not as—"

Lucas's page flipping picked up again. "So who was that guy?" he interrupted abruptly.

"Excuse me?"

Lucas had halted mid-Quad. The quick and the tardy surrounded us. It was understandable. We were this radiant American teen couple, perfectly toned, coiffed, and ensembled. Icons of accessible popularity. But it was way annoying nevertheless. Fans swirled around us.

"The one who was sucking on your fist," Lucas said, and there was this collective gasp.

I turned to the stalled crowd. "Excuse us, please. This is so not a public moment. And"—I glanced at my TagHeuer timepiece—"I believe the punctuality-obsessed Principal Lehman will be touring the campus right about now."

Our audience rapidly dispersed. Still, it took me a moment to decipher Lucas's question. "Sucking on my fist?"

"Nibbling your knuckles, laying lips on your limbs. That guy in the leather jacket who was kissing your hand."

"Raphael?" My heart lurched. Lucas's azure eyes searched mine for reassurance. It was so moving. "He's just the new boy in our class. Of course you wouldn't know him," I realized. "He's years younger than you."

"So, are you going to the Monster Bash with him?" Lucas handed me my book.

"With Raphael? As if," I countered hotly, pushing the volume back at him. "He's a low-end high school boy, and I am so not a babysitter! I have standards, Lucas. I mean, you have to at least have a valid driver's license."

"Then would you go with me?" my hockey hunk queried.

"Are you asking or taking a survey?" I demanded.

"Cher, I've been trying to catch up with you for days to ask. Will you go to the Monster Bash with me?"

I did the *Cosmopolitan* magazine count. You keep

your eyes fastened on his. Which was a brutal piece of cake. Because just then Lucas's orbs were the thrilling steely blue of a timber wolf's. Then you smile discreetly and you silently go, like one one thousand, two one thousand, three one thousand. And then, very softly, you say, "Of course."

"Excellent," Lucas said, returning my algebra book once more. "I'll beep you later, okay?"

"Of course," I whispered again in my throaty *Cosmo* manner.

On the wings of victory, I sailed through the school day. And at four o'clock, I was curled up in the window seat of our Beverly Hills mansionette reading Mary Shelley's *Frankenstein*.

The girl could write. In fact, her description of Victor's early years—that was the infamous Dr. Frankenstein's first name, Victor—was deeply absorbing. Let me say this, the book actually starts out with letters from a guy named R. Walton to his sister. Walton is this educated young adventurer, traveling by ship in the ice-jammed far reaches of the world. Suddenly, in the gray and frigid Arctic, R. Walton sees this humongous creature riding in a dog sled across these glaciers. The man or thing, whatever it is, disappears among the icy mountains. And that's that. Sort of.

Because later R., or Robert, Walton finds this completely despairing, near-dead guy who is trying to catch up with that very creature. And, of course, the desperate frostbitten wretch turns out to be Victor Frankenstein, and then he starts to tell his story.

I put down the book and stood up and sort of shook myself. I hadn't even gotten to the scary parts yet, but I was all jittery and grossed. That is the power of excellent storytelling.

I mean, here I was in our frantically pastel palace, and I still felt all clammy and cold. It was like I was out on that creaky old ship waiting for Victor to launch into his life story. Which supposedly would reveal how he and the mammoth iceman intersected.

So when Josh stuck his head into the library and went, "Cher, you've got company," I brutally freaked.

"What's the matter with you?" my observant stepbrother asked.

"Nothing! Why?" I demanded.

"Well, let's see. You're pale as a ghost, you jumped about a foot in the air, and if you continue hyperventilating like that you'll probably need one of your Neiman bags to breath into."

"It's this dumb story you recommended," I grumbled, pointing an accusatory juliette at the culprit volume. "It's got me totally spooked and I haven't even gotten to Frankenstein's childhood yet."

Josh grinned proudly. "That's why it's a classic," he said. "You want to see your friend with the safety pin or should I send for EMS?"

"Why don't you keep feeding Daddy ice cream and clotted fat and then we can order up EMS for two?" I snapped at him. But I was thinking: Safety pin? Could Sharon Clay be at my door? "This safety pin, is it like connected to a person?" I asked.

"Dermatologically," Josh said. "She says she's a friend from school."

I rushed past him, out of the library. "You're welcome," the so-not-my-bro called after me.

In our soaring domed entry hall, Sharon was shifting

her weight from one combat-ready foot to the other. Her straw hair was bunched up in a knot from which peroxide-yellow stalks exploded. Little metal skulls hung from tiny chains in two of the several holes in her earlobes. Plus a spiked leather collar that looked as if it had been swiped from a rabid Doberman graced her neck. Oh, yes. And the safety pin was in place, puncturing the inflamed patch of skin above her eye.

"Sharon," I greeted her. "What a surprise."

"I'm probably interrupting you," she said, taking in the opulence of our surroundings. "I probably shouldn't really even have come, but—" She shrugged her shoulders and one of the straps of her pale thrift-shop shift fell. Tugging it back up, she briefly met my eyes. "Cher, I'm desperate," she confessed. "And you're the only one who can help me."

My surprise instantly gave way to a flood of compassion for the forlorn femme. "Of course," I said. "Let's talk." Leading Sharon to the library, I called to Lucy, "We've got company, Luce. Can you fix us a tray of hors d'oeuvres?"

"Later," came the reply from the kitchen. "That girl whose husband made her dress up like Tom Cruise is fighting with her mother on Sally Jessy."

"Excuse me, Sharon," I said, pressing the button that lit the faux flames in our fireplace. "Lucy's a gem, really. But she's a furious talk show freak. I'll just be a minute," I assured her on my way out the door. "I'll have Luce whip us up something simple. Low-cal, air-popped popcorn. Maybe some carrot sticks. A veggie chip or two." I headed for the kitchen.

Lucy was perched where I knew she'd be, on one of the aluminum stools facing the countertop TV. From the set, a girl with huge, crimped hair was shouting at a woman with way too much eyeliner, "You were my mother. You should've looked out for me!"

Between bites of cheese nachos, Lucy was nodding in agreement. And she was wearing sunglasses that looked extremely like the monster Webs I'd misplaced a week ago.

"Lucy, we have a guest," I announced, silencing the big-haired raver with a click of the remote. "I'd like some snacks, please. And Diet Cokes. And why are you wearing my sunglasses?"

"That poor girl," Lucy commiserated, then spun to face me. "Because I've been getting headaches ever since you fixed the kitchen, and my optometrist says it's the glare. I was thinking of suing, but Dr. Weissman knows your father and he said I'd probably lose the case."

"Daddy is a vicious opponent," I agreed. "Anyway, I'm thinking of redoing this room." Prepared to return to Sharon, I started for the door.

"Wait! You didn't even ask me how the tofu seminar was," Lucy complained.

"Oh, Luce. I'm sorry. How was it?" I said.

"Don't ask," she grumbled.

Sharon stood abruptly as I entered the library. "I shouldn't have come," she began apologizing again. "It's just that I have nowhere else to turn."

"I like to think of myself as a first rather than a last resort," I confided. "But as long as you're here, why not fill me in on the issue. Two heads are always better than one. Not cosmetically, of course. I'm just speaking metaphorically."

"You are so generous, aren't you?" There it was again, that strange hint of sarcasm. But it was hard to take personally the ill-tempered tones of a poorly pierced woman. "Everyone likes you. Everyone thinks you are so classic," Sharon went on, her voice rising emotionally. "Like you're this major paradigm of a Beverly Hills Betty. I have no choice—"

The girl was getting way dramatic. Suddenly, she threw herself onto our overstuffed silk sofa and covered her face with her hands. Her shoulders began to shake, slip straps shimmying perilously close to the plunging point. "I want to be like you," Sharon blurted unexpectedly.

"For real?" I said. It was not unusual that someone wanted to emulate me. That's what being a role model is all about. But the passionate nature of Sharon's plea took me by surprise.

"Ferociously for real," she wailed.

Drawn as much by the tumultuous emotional level as by my request for hors d'oeuvres, Lucy appeared at the library door. She glanced at the blank television screen and seemed disappointed to discover only a live drama in progress. "You like tofu?" she asked Sharon.

Startled, Sharon shook her emulsion-starved head.

"Me neither," Lucy confessed, "but it's a very versatile food. Like Play Doh, only half the calories. You can make practically anything out of it." On the coffee table before us, she set down a platter of what looked so like high-cal cookies. "Anyway, we were out of carrots and Diet Coke. So here's the highlight of the 'Wonderful World of Tofu' seminar. We call it Tofus Ahoy."

"Wow, Luce!" I exclaimed, frantically flipped at the authentic cookie look of her creation. "These are the bomb. They look brutally bona fide. Major snaps to you!"

Lucy shrugged and left us.

"Try one." I offered the plate to Sharon.

Fireplace flames glinted off the spikes of her leather necklace as she shook her head no. "I should never have come," she announced, wringing her hands, which, I noted, were crucially in need of radical skin and nail care. "I'm sorry to have taken your time, Cher. I know you're busy and popular and like you have a gazillion more important things to do—"

"An observation here," I stopped her. "You frantically overapologize, Sharon. And while I'm a major fan of politeness, it works best in moderation. You don't want to push it all the way to groveling, which is so unattractive. Also," I added, snagging one of Lucy's tofu cookies, "I happen to be free this afternoon, so your stopping by is no problemo. I wasn't really doing anything, just reading this excellently creepy book for Mr. Hall's class."

As Sharon reviewed my comments, I bit cautiously into the cookie. Tscha! It perfectly captured the crunchy chocolate chip richness of its calorie-crammed namesake. I was so psyched that I'd signed Lucy up for the tofu seminar. I felt fiercely justified. Josh could eat his words, while I gorged on no-cal Tofus Ahoy.

"Girlfriend, you really should try these," I encouraged Sharon, reaching for seconds. "Next to aerobic exercise, a well-planned pig-out is an excellent mood-changer. And that's one of the first things we'll want to focus on in your makeover. Developing an upbeat attitude. Without which not even a beaded Badgley Mischka sparkles—"

"My makeover? Then you'll do it?" Sharon enthused.

"It's already begun," I pointed out, happy to hear excitement energize the girl's formerly glum monotone. Hope is so enlivening.

"You'll help me to become—" She paused and watched me munch my tofu for a moment. Then, reaching for a cookie of her own, she finished her question: "—a brutally popular, Demi-toned, Cameron-cute Betty just like you?" she said.

As she bit into the cookie, I studied her. The safety pin, biker, and pet shop jewelry would have to go, of course. And hair repair was a frantic priority. Out of the color swatches streaking Sharon's head, we would choose one, at most two, shades of blond to work with. The rest, while not easy, was so doable. But what really impressed me was how well the girl was able to imitate the way I ate. Scarfing style is as unique as fingerprints, yet Sharon had fully duplicated my munching manner. It was an excellent sign.

"I can't believe this is tofu," she was saying. "Can I get the recipe?"

"I'm sure we can get Luce to E-mail or fax it to your housekeeper," I said.

"Whoops, I totally forgot," Sharon went, scrambling to her feet. "I'm supposed to pick up a bundle of filets for Melba at Wilshire Meats."

I saw the panic in her soft brown eyes, which, I noticed for the first time, were tigerishly flecked with these attractive specks of yellow. Which a café au lait shadow would furiously accent. "You'll make it. They don't close for hours," I said, standing, too. "Come on, I'll walk you to the door."

"When do we begin?" she asked in the entry hall. "Should I come back later?"

"Not even. There's tons of planning involved in a truly decent makeover. And that part is essentially a lonely job," I explained, opening the front door. "We'll talk," I promised as Sharon headed down our cobblestoned circular drive to the chauffeured Benz waiting at the curb. "A word of caution," I called. "However tasty the occasional burger may be, I'd try to limit red meat intake. It's a major poundage enhancer."

"Oh, the steaks aren't for me," she responded reassuringly. "They're for my dad. He's a committed carnivore."

At least we had this in common, I mused. Nodding knowingly, I waved goodbye as Sharon's Mercedes headed south along our tree-lined boulevard.

A makeover! There is nothing I enjoy more than bettering a peer's quality of life. Except, maybe, maxing out my Gold card on a mall run with De. Upon reentry, I fell back against our massive front door and went, "Yesss!"

Mom's portrait was looking way approving. "So, Ma, you jammin' activist," I said, "you are my total inspiration. Daddy told me what a down humanitarian you were, and how committed to environmental issues. Like how you totally stopped wearing fur the minute you found out you might be allergic." I gave Mom a thumbs-up and hurried back to the library.

There was so much to do. If time had permitted, I'd have shot some Polaroids of Sharon. In addition to offering me a realistic record of her restructuring needs, I'd have used them to show my client how her sagging shoulders and hunched presentation cut crucial supermodel inches from her height, creating this bitter illusion of defeat. Which is such a lame look. But I hadn't snapped pics, so I needed to jot down and sketch as much information as I could remember.

My duty to Sharon was at war with my impulse to speed dial De and tell her what had just happened. She'd totally plotz! Thinking of De reminded me that she'd talked Murray into driving her to the bookstore after school to pick up a copy of *Frankenstein*. Which reminded me that there were only about a million pages of the shudder-inducing tale left for me to read.

Sketch pad in hand, I stared at the faux flames leaping in the grill. A makeover was serious business and ferociously beneficial to others. Whereas reading *Frankenstein* was all about getting a def grade in English, which seemed brutally selfish by comparison. I was just sitting there wondering how I could condense the reading experience to allow me the time I needed for helping Sharon, when in walked Cliff Notes in denim. The step-know-it-all, Josh.

The moment I glanced at him, he crumpled something he was holding and guiltily stuffed it into his jeans pocket. "Oh," he said. "I heard the door slam and thought you'd gone out." Then he spotted Lucy's cookies and, giving me this conspiratorial grin, wandered over to the sofa and helped himself to one.

"And you came in here looking for what, new ways to endanger Daddy's health?" Josh couldn't have known how tofu the excellent cookies actually were. "And anyway," I began my pitch, "how can I go out when I have all this work to do?"

"Did your friend leave?" He frantically ignored the bait and, looking over my shoulder, glanced at my preliminary notes on Sharon.

"I should have guessed," Josh said, shaking his head all judgmental. "That poor girl with the safety pin is your new victim, isn't she?"

"Victim?" I responded angrily.

"Okay. Candidate for improvement, if you prefer."

"It's not a matter of my preferences," I snapped. "Did

you even see the girl? I suppose you'd let a friend of yours walk around Jurassically attired, wearing totally toadhead clothes. But look who I'm talking to," I added, gazing pointedly at the basic denim and flannel uniform Josh affected. "I've seen you plummet from Banana Republic to Gap to Old Navy."

The boy plopped down beside me and reached for another cookie.

"You'll be way depressed to discover those are actually healthy," I taunted.

"Oh, really?"

I didn't like his tone, which kind of matched mine. "Anyway, Josh," I said, lightening up, trying to get us back on track, "I don't see why you're so negative about my aiding a fellow human being. I thought you college people were brutally into changing the world and helping others."

"You don't get it, do you?" he said. Which, of course, is everyone's favorite thing to hear. But I forced myself to smile and to blink innocently and try to look all, No, Josh. Oh, please explain to clueless little me how the world really works. And inside I was all, As if!

"Helping others doesn't mean changing them into what *you* think is fashionable and popular and perfect. Cher, why are you always tinkering with other people's lives, trying to fix them whether they're broken or not? Can't you find any area in which *you* need help?"

Under other circumstances, this would have been an excellent moment to inform Lecture Man that Sharon had asked me, even begged me, to transform her. But I had more urgent business.

"Don't be a stooge, Josh. Of course I need help." I saw my opening and leaped in. "While I have an excellent collection of magazines and books on tape, I'm not as compulsive a reader as you. You read stuff that isn't even assigned. You've even read and recommended this spooky tale that I'm doing a book report on. So you see, I do so value your input. I viciously love this book, although it is extremely eerie and written in somewhat dated prose. Which you, being so much older and wiser, probably don't have a problem with. Whereas, it's not exactly easy for people of my generation to fully comprehend. I mean, I am way surprised at how much philosophical and scientific chat is stuck into this story."

Josh was smiling. He was regarding me with this benevolent, brotherly amusement. Tscha! I had bitterly played the boy. My mission was moments from completion.

"That's a very perceptive observation," Josh decided. Switching to nerd mode, he went into this rant about how young people of Mary Shelley's time were majorly infatuated with scientific breakthroughs and were always debating these deep issues about how men of science would change the universe.

"Men of science?" I observed.

"I meant people, of course," he politically corrected himself. "Men *and* women. In fact, Victor Frankenstein," Josh elaborated, "was that kind of person. A student who got hooked on science and started believing that he could do anything, even create a new human being. Which reminds me of a certain contemporary person," he announced, eyes angelically fixed on the beamed ceiling of the library, "who so believes in the power of cosmetic transformation that she does all these weird experiments. Her goals, she thinks, are benevolent. She's only trying to improve her species. So she fixes, meddles, tinkers, and advises, trying to create, you might say, new and better beings—just as poor Victor did."

"Oh, really?" I replied, in this furiously innocent tone. I was not going to react to Josh's lame insults and lose sight of my ultimate goal, which was to get him to summarize the Frankenstein saga for me. He was doing a fair job so far, but I needed more details. "Why do you say, poor Victor? I mean, what happened to the boy?" I pressed.

"It's all in the book. Don't you want to find out for yourself?" Josh asked, gobbling yet another cookie.

"May I be frank?" I decided to move to a more direct approach. "I have to say I agree with you that self-improvement is a worthy goal—"

He was nodding in agreement. They say if you get the first yes, you're halfway home. And they are so right.

"And writing a righteous paper on this total classic will much improve my English grade—"

Yes number two was being nodded as I spoke.

"And all I need is like a teensy bit of assistance. And you know how hard it is for me to ask because I'm basically so self-sufficient. And anyway, there are so few people I need things from. And right now you are like among that ferociously select group."

"Are you asking me to help you with **your** assignment?" Josh finally got it.

"Well, yeah. Just a little. I mean, I **don't want** you to write my paper or anything. Just, **like, do you** think you could fill me in on the story?"

"Is that all?" he said, with this **little smirk.** "Okay, well, basically, Victor's fatal flaw is believing that he can control what he creates. And he does succeed in creating this 'improved' being. But the monster he made viciously turns on him." Josh lapsed into amused silence.

"Oh, excuse me," I said. "For a moment I thought actual help would be forthcoming. But what do I get instead? A bitter lecture on the perils of betterment."

Josh was chuckling, which was not just annoying, but totally fueled my fury.

"So like I'm supposed to see what happened when poor Victor Frankenstein, this total science dweeb, went on an improvement spree," I continued. "And then what? Get all nervous about what might happen to me, who has not a dweeb bone in my excellently toned bod, if I do a makeover on Sharon—who, unlike Frankenstein's monster, actually begged for my help? And, speaking of help, forgive me for thinking you might take my needs seriously and actually deliver the assistance I requested."

Tscha! Josh was comfortingly contrite. "I'm sorry. Honest, Cher," he said. "I didn't mean to blow off your request."

But I was way wound up and couldn't stop. I seized on the next weapon at hand. "And those cookies you've been gorging happen to be made of tofu!" I raged.

Josh stood abruptly. But instead of turning green and spewing, he reached into his pocket and pulled out the crumpled object he'd hidden earlier. He dropped it onto the coffee table before me. The balled-up bag opened slowly, spewing crumbs across the polished table surface.

"What is that?" I shrieked.

"The empty chocolate chip cookie bag I found in the kitchen," Josh replied. "I only came in here to snag a snack."

"I don't understand," I gasped. But the truth was dawning painfully. "You mean . . . Lucy dumped a sack of store-bought sweets on us? Generic million-calorie cookies that you can buy by the case at like Vons?"

Josh nodded, and I brutally choked. How many cookies had I inhaled? Two, three? I'd thought I could chomp fearlessly. Now, if my calculations were correct, I'd need like three step classes and two spins to work off the glut. I hid my face in my hands, devastated.

And then, through the ringing in my ears, I heard Josh's apologetic voice. "Cher, are you okay? Is there anything I can do to help?"

I looked up. "Well, yes, actually," I said. "Could you like summarize the book for me?"

Chapter 5

*S*uccess has its price. On Friday morning, through bleary, sleep-deprived eyes, I watched the glowing numbers on my bedside digital shift from six fifty-nine to seven. Unable to wait another moment, I speed dialed Dionne from bed.

Getting Josh to tell me the Frankenstein tale had saved me reading hours and eyestrain, but I hadn't counted on Josh being such a ferociously fine story-teller. His rendition of the ancient horror tale was so def that it left me fully spooked. I had a brutal time falling asleep.

Of course, Lucy's faux tofu treats didn't help. Sugar makes me fiercely manic. So, awesomely energized, I tossed and turned. But trying to calculate the poundage price I'd pay for Lucy's little deception just kept my mind whirring. Even after I decided to shelve the obesity equation, I was still vaguely zoned—and majorly bummed.

No surprise there. I mean, in terms of vicious disasters, Victor Frankenstein's botched endeavor made Amber's ensemble experiments look triumphant.

According to Josh's summary, Vic had started out surrounded by all these excellent people: a loving dad, an adorable little brother, a true-blue friend named Henry Clerval, and this bright, brutally compassionate Betty of a stepsister, who was actually adopted by the kindhearted Frankensteins, and so not really related to Victor. "Sort of like us," Josh had suggested. To which I'd silently replied, As if!

But once Vic was off to college and getting pumped on scientific theories and falling into this obsession about creating a living being, his life took a rapid dive.

Even now, with sunlight streaming through the flattering, sheer pink curtains in my bedroom, I shuddered thinking of it. My knuckles tightened on the telephone receiver as I listened to De's cellular ring and ring. But her mobile was either turned off or buried in the depths of her furry backpack. So I hung up and dialed her home phone. After four rings, De's answering machine picked up. Which meant I had to listen to this week's original rap composition by Murray, with Sean making these record-scratching, spit-up sounds in the background.

"Girlfriend, where are you? Help, it's me," I urged at concert's end. "Call me back. I'm taking my Motorola into the shower with me."

Clutching my cell phone, I stumbled toward the bathroom. I was wiped out, but nothing compared to Victor Frankenstein, I mused. He'd been like totally obsessed. Each night, he'd labor alone in secret. Which, naturally, left him all pale and irritable. And he'd forget to eat. Plus he practically canceled the fresh air and exercise portion of his day. All of which dealt a severe blow to his social life and was reminiscent of Daddy's workaholic mode. At least Daddy scrambled into a designer suit and caught a few healing rays between exiting his limo and entering his law office. Poor Victor's outings were executed under cover of darkness and took him to like cemeteries and morgues.

In my Calvin boxers and classic white T, I caught a glimpse of myself in my mirrored bathroom wall. Sleeplessness had distorted my features. Fear had frizzed my locks. Like the monster Frankenstein finally succeeded in creating, I looked like death warmed over.

The subdued jingle of my cellular jump-started my heart. I fumbled for the phone and clicked on talk mode.

"You rang?" De's upbeat voice did more to restore my natural glow than a hydrating peel-off facial mask and a moisturizing shampoo with cleansing conditioners combined.

"Girlfriend, I have so much to discuss," I confided. "Guess which ensembly clueless classmate showed up at my maison yesterday afternoon wanting a full-scale, major makeover. I was so moved—"

"I can't believe it," De squealed. "Amber has come to her senses, at last!"

"Right," I remarked. "And the cast of *Friends* said they'd do the show for free next season. Not even! Anyway, De," I reminded her, "I said *wanting* a make-over, not needing one. How close are you to departure time?"

"Twenty minutes, give or take. But I can put you on speakerphone while I hot roll my hair, okay?"

"I'll floss and shower and call you right back," I said. "Did you pick up the book last night?"

"Which book?" De wanted to know.

"Duh," I grunted, taking the fluoride toothpaste with whitening agents out of my cabinet. "Well, I guess it's not our close personal friend Ariel Stein or the renowned author R. L. Stine," I hinted.

"Oh, you mean *Frankenstein?*" De guessed. "Murray decided to stop at Blockbuster before we went to the bookstore, so I picked up the video instead. We watched it last night. Eeeww! As the monster, De Niro was totally gross."

"You watched the video?" I admonished, phone crooked in my shoulder, toothpaste tube poised above my brush. "We're supposed to be doing a book report."

"Whoops, my bad." De giggled. "Did you start reading it yet?"

"As if!" I exclaimed. "I got Josh to fill me in on the vital plot details."

"Excellent!" De applauded my ploy. "But, Cher, you didn't tell me who requested the makeover."

"Initials *S.C.,*" I enticed her. "More later. Right now I've got to brush away my mouth fuzzies, mousse my coif, and choose a perfect Friday outfit. Back to you in ten, girlfriend," I said, and clicked off.

For nine of those promised ten minutes, I busily prepared for a shining school day. But standing before the rotating rack of my walk-in closet, last night's story returned to haunt me. My grip tightened on the creamy leather jeans I'd chosen to go with my ribbed, silk knit halter top. And once more I heard Josh describing how

Victor Frankenstein's creation got totally bent out of shape.

It was because the monster longed for love. But just the sight of him made everyone want to bail, Josh had asserted. Plus the monster's frustration tolerance was way low. Which made it hard for him to have quality relationships.

I pulled my selections from the rotating rack and slipped into the finely made merchandise. A moment later, sitting before my dressing table, spritzing and taming my wild blond locks, I again considered the monster's plight.

First, he begged Frankenstein to make him a mate, someone he could talk to and love. If not, he threatened to destroy all that Victor cherished. So, Vic went, sure, no problem, he'd rob a few graves, sew up another being, and "animate" her. Animation, back then, meant jolting someone or something with the awesome natural force of electricity. It had nothing to do with Ren and Stimpy.

But Vic was lying. He definitely did not want to set another angry monster loose upon the land. Which, right there, kind of sealed the fates of his father, his little brother, and poor Elizabeth, the faithful, warm-hearted adopted sister whom Frankenstein frantically adored.

My cell phone rang and I jumped. The pink scrunchie I was about to wrap around my locks shot from my hand, nearly knocking over my petite sample flask of Pleasure.

"Sharon Clay?" De shrieked, when I answered the call. "Sharon of the hair of a thousand blonds asked you for a makeover?"

"Begged," I suggested. "I'll fill you in at the bean bar in the Quad, okay?"

"Definitely," De agreed. "Let's synchronize our Movados."

"I'm wearing my yellow band Swatch today," I told her. "But I'll be there at the stroke of eight-thirty. Order me a decaf capp if you arrive first."

"Two percent milk?" she asked.

I thought of the high-cal cookies I'd innocently scarfed yesterday. "Skim," I said sadly, and clicked off.

Amber was sitting with De when I arrived at the school coffee bar. She was wearing this fringed pony-skin vest over a tie-dyed T-shirt, and she was slurping down foam, spooning it off the top of a mug of coffee.

"Milk mustache," I said, by way of greeting. "And it goes so well with that retro, swingin' London, Beatles-era white lipstick and fringe look."

"Yuck!" Amber wiped her upper lip, then inspected the napkin. "You lied," she accused me.

"Psych out," I said.

She shoved the cup toward me vengefully. "Well, it's your cappuccino," she gloated. I waited for her to say "Psych back," but she didn't. Instead, she got up in a huff, grabbed her quilted Chanel handbag and bunny backpack, wiggled her iridescent-white enameled nails at De, and left.

"You let her eat my foam?" I accused De.

"I was distracted," she confessed. "Murray and Sean showed up just as I set down our cups. They were all into cackles and whispers. They've got some random surprise brewing which, of course, they *so* could not share with Amber and me." De rolled her hazel eyes. "Here, take my foam." She began spooning it into my cup. "Miles forgot again and gave me cinnamon."

"Which I totally love," I said. "I forgive you. But don't tell anyone that I accepted secondhand cinnamon from you or sipped used latte foam, okay?"

"Never," De pledged. She patted the seat beside her, then tore her buttery croissant in half. "Want some?"

Regretfully, I shook my head, no. "Lucy succumbed to this major midlife crisis yesterday. When I requested a healthy snack, she slipped me fraudulent cookies. They were supposed to be tofu, but they were totally mock. A generically mass-produced brand."

"Heinous," De gasped, and laid a buttery yet sympathetic hand on mine. "How many calories?"

"I can't go there, De."

"My bad. Forgive me," she said, then stuffed this big puffy chunk of croissant into her mouth.

"And Josh was in on it," I grumbled, turning away from the sight of her ecstatic munching. "Plus he was issuing these dire warnings about me trying to improve Sharon. Even though she bitterly solicited my aid. And," I continued, outraged, "he kept hinting that there were all these brutal parallels between me and Victor Frankenstein."

"Oh, you mean, because both of you are like so committed to bettering things?"

"Well, I guess that's part of it," I acknowledged.

"And like you both have this defiant determination, this deep conviction, that your way is the best way."

"I'm a basically self-confident person, if that's what you mean," I agreed.

"No matter what anyone else tries to tell you—"

"Excuse me, Dionne," I found myself sharply interrupting her. "What are you trying to say?"

"Well, in the movie," De explained, brushing flaky bits of croissant from her Dior-bronzed lips, "Frankenstein's t.b. bud, Henry Clerval, is always trying to stop him from experimenting. And Victor makes this speech. And when we were listening to it last night, Murray said, 'That sounds just like you.' And I said, 'Not even! That is so Cher.'"

"Really?" I said coolly. "And do you think you could like condense the speech for me?" I asked, suddenly determined not to mention the pastry flake clinging to her cheek.

"Oh, sure," Dionne said cheerfully. "Victor says, 'We can change things. We can make things better. We are on the verge of undreamt-of discoveries.' You know, that kind of upbeat attitude. Maybe that's what Josh meant," she suggested.

"Actually, that boy who tries to pass himself off as my brother," I said, picking at a few fallen crumbs of croissant, "tried to insinuate that what happened to Frankenstein would happen to me."

"And that is?" De asked.

"Only that Frankenstein's monster was viciously unappreciative of the new, improved life he'd been given. And what did Victor get for all his grave robbing and corpse stitching? Just this ungrateful creature who totally turned on him." I licked the croissant flakes off my fingertips.

"So what does that mean, that Sharon's going to bite the hand that removes her safety pin? I don't think so," De said supportively. "Anyway, Cher, Sharon is nothing like Frankenstein's monster. I mean, that poor creature was pieced together from dead parts."

"And Sharon isn't?" I replied. "Have you even seen her hair? I mean, it'll take a lot more than hot oil conditioners to bring those bleached follicles back to life."

My work was cut out for me. I knew I'd have to spend most of the weekend plotting Sharon's makeover. I spotted the candidate herself just before fifth period. Lucas and I had been dawdling in the corridor near my locker, when I saw Sharon heading for Ms. Hanratty's room.

She was wearing this nubby thrift-shop sweater over a faded silk camisole. I was pleased to note, however, that she'd traded her spiked canine collar for a simple chain. Okay, it looked as if it was made of steel and strong enough to keep a bike from being stolen, but I felt it was a step in the right direction.

"Will you excuse me, Lucas?" I said. "There's someone I've got to catch up with before the bell rings."

"No problem." He buzzed my cheek and shouldered his backpack. "I've gotta get changed for practice anyway. So, you want to hit a show in Westwood tomorrow night?"

"Oh, I'd love to," I said, biting my lip as I quickly thought over the excellent offer. "I'm just not sure. This weekend's looking brutally booked."

Lucas's dazzling smile wavered briefly. Then he shrugged his massive shoulders, said, "I'll call you," and took off down the hall.

I hurried toward Hanratty's room. I was peeking inside, signaling for Sharon to join me in the corridor, when someone tugged on my teddy-bear backpack. I whirled to face the culprit.

"Hey, princess." Raphael's boyish grin went a long

way toward deflating my annoyance. "What're you doing next week, say Friday P.M.?" he asked.

"Going to the Monster Bash with Lucas." The words were on the tip of my tongue, but someone else's lips had uttered them. Startled, Raph and I both turned to find Sharon standing in the classroom doorway.

"It's true," I confirmed, gently placing a consoling hand on the sleeve of his stellar jacket.

"Lucas is a senior," Sharon added. "A frantically sought-after jock, representing our school as Mr. July in the new Hockey Hunks calendar. Plus, he's got a driver's license. He drives a Porsche——"

Raphael's grin was melting like a scented mood candle in a sauna.

"Sharon," I interrupted. "Can we talk? Raph, will you excuse us, please."

As the somewhat stunned hottie nodded yes and began to back away, Sharon annotated her mini-biography of Lucas. "And he doesn't usually date down," she called after Raphael.

"Excuse me? What does that mean?" I demanded.

"Duh, what a 'tard I am," the girl quickly repented. "I meant, age-wise, Lucas being a senior and all. How furiously inarticulate am I?"

I took a deep breath. "Look," I said. The bell was about to ring and I had to get to social studies. "I've been going over my schedule, and I think I'll be ready for the makeover on Sunday afternoon. Does that work for you?"

"Well, I was hoping we could start sooner——"

"Sharon, you have no idea the planning and work a successful makeover requires," I pointed out, trying to restrain the impatience in my tone. "We're not talking about sitting on a stool at some department store counter while a gum-chewing cosmetician breathes spearmint-scented tobacco breath in your face while she reshapes your eyebrows. We're talking about transformation."

The bell rang. We both jumped. "Sunday, then?" I said.

"Will I be home in time for *America's Funniest Home Videos?*" she asked.

Chapter 6

*F*riday evening I was home alone, doing Sharon's color chart. Well, I wasn't entirely alone. Daddy and Josh were downstairs, going over these legal depositions with a crew of law clerks from Daddy's office. I glimpsed them from the door to the den on the way to my room. The clerks were like Santa's helpers. They were all dressed alike, wearing red suspenders with these crisp white shirts. Their striped ties were loosened, shirt sleeves neatly rolled, collars unbuttoned. Josh, of course, was attired in sweats and sneakers. Your basic Grinch.

"Cher," he hollered from the bottom of our elegantly winding marble staircase, "Dionne's trying to call you."

It was eight o'clock. Lucas had phoned at five. With all the prep necessary for Sharon's makeover, I'd reluctantly turned down his movie offer. At five-twenty, I'd blown off a major mall hop with De. De's invitation was interrupted by a call-waiting plea from Tai to review the crushed velvet outfit her mother was making her wear to this bar mitzvah in Bel Air. I explained to Tai that I didn't have a moment to spare, then got back to De, who graciously volunteered to appraise Tai's ensemble. The minute I hung up, Kimberly Woo buzzed saying she was rethinking her Elvira decision and did I think she should cut her hair and try to go to the Bash as Jamie Lee Curtis? I thought it was a radical move and deserved further thought. Which I so couldn't give it this weekend.

Ten minutes later Murray called to say that he and Sean were collecting hair extensions, and did I have any I could lend them. I didn't even check my tufted silk accessory box or bother to ask why they wanted used hair. I told Murray to try me again early next week.

Amber beeped around six and begged me to attend the premiere of her new hockey cheer. She'd pressured four pep team freshmen into performing the piece at Jesse Fiegenhut's father's recording studio. And, of course, she could so not understand why the debut of her cheer was not priority one on my weekend to-do list.

And that was all before dinner, which Lucy served wearing my sunglasses. She came reeling out of the kitchen wheeling the mahogany serving cart, which she brutally rammed into our antique white French Provincial sideboard.

"Oh, I am so sorry, Luce," I murmured sarcastically. "Is kitchen glare still bothering your eyes?"

Daddy and Josh were in lawful conversation at the time and way oblivious to Lucy's dramatic stumbling and bumping act.

"And what are we having tonight, tofu lamb chops?" I whispered harshly as she presented our entrée.

"You said you'd fix the kitchen," Lucy countered,

spooning a steaming heap of my favorite garlic mashed potatoes onto the tablecloth next to my plate.

I chose to ignore her petulance. My energy had to be preserved for the task ahead. So after dinner, wary of further distractions, I had silenced both my cellular and the pale pink console phone in my bedroom.

After Josh's announcement about De trying to reach me, I opened the door to my room and hollered, "Josh, please take a message. I can't be interrupted."

"Cher, De says she's been trying you for more than an hour."

"Jo-osh," I responded, "I've been trying to get some crucial work done since I got home from school. Please, tell her that I'll get back to her the second I have a free minute."

But I didn't return De's call. I slaved over Sharon's color chart. Then, with a fresh legal pad and my pink feather pen at the ready, I popped on my headphones and began transcribing vital transformational tips from my collection of self-help books on tape.

I must have dozed off. I awoke with a start sometime later to some diet guru's rant about the dire consequences of not guzzling eight glasses of water a day. Exhausted, I removed the earplugs, shut off the tape, and fell back onto my bed.

Saturday was practically a repeat performance. Lucy was off. I dragged my weary bod downstairs and fixed myself a bowl of bran with skim milk, wisely deciding against the additional carbo-load of banana slices.

The gleaming surfaces of our renovated kitchen seemed far more alive than I. Plus, sunlight sparkling off all that metal made me furiously wince. Then— tscha!—fate stepped in. I spied my very own Web shades lying on the aluminum work counter beside the television set. I put them on, poured a glass of fresh-squeezed orange juice for Daddy, and left it for him on the counter beside two Flintstone chewables and a host of other nutritional supplements. Then, cereal bowl in hand, I schlepped upstairs to continue my prep work.

It was midafternoon when I heard a pounding at our front door, punctuated by a multiple sounding of chimes. Reluctantly, I roused myself.

On the way downstairs, I realized that I'd forgotten to shower. I'd planned to do it immediately after sucking up the bran and had actually gotten as far as choosing an aloe vera foaming bath botanical over the freesia shower gelée, when the sight of my lucite makeup tray inspired me to review Sharon's cosmetic needs. One makeover thing led to another.

Now, catching a glimpse of myself in the hall mirror, I furiously freaked. Not only was I makeup free, but I was still wearing my Webs and the ankle-length smiley face T-shirt I'd slipped into last night. Plus my hair was all frizz city.

The front door chimes continued to sound. I ran my fingers through my unruly hair, took a deep breath, and opened the door. And my best friend went, "Eeeww!"

"Oh, that's a nice greeting, De," I admonished.

In this choice hot pink vinyl mini and matching hat, with a caramel crop-top that displayed her faux navel ring, De was on the veranda staring at me, wide eyed. "What happened to you?" she gasped.

"Excuse me?" I said. "Did you stop by just to hurl insults or was there something you wanted? I'm in the midst of planning my most golden makeover ever, and I simply lost track of time."

"And shampoo and makeup and daywear and shoes—"

"I've got to get back to my room," I interrupted her inventory. "Call me later, De."

She stuck a Capezio pump in the door, blocking my attempt to close it. "Cher, I've been trying to reach you all day," she protested, "by cell phone, E-mail, station-to-station, and beeper. Girlfriend, I'm desperate."

"Well, if you think you can speak to me and keep your lunch down, too," I retorted, opening the door and allowing her to enter. "I've just got so much to do."

"I know," she said. "And I wouldn't have bothered you—"

"Dionne," I cut her off, "do you realize the awesome challenge that lies before me? I mean, Sharon Clay is renowned for her eccentric dress code, egregious tactlessness, and overall loser ambiance."

"And her posture totally bites," De added supportively.

"Exactly. I mean," I mused, suddenly inspired, "just think of her last name."

"Clay?" De said, following me through the entry hall into our way spacious living room.

I flung myself onto the sprawling sectional sofa, pulled a silk brocade pillow from behind my back, and hugged it to my chest. "What does it remind you of? Just think about it," I encouraged.

"Okay. Clay," De said uncertainly, dropping into the comfy club chair across the way. "What, like making hand plaques in kindergarten? That kind of clay?"

"Bingo!" I said. "Clay is basically this dull, clammy, earthbound substance. But also fully changeable. Don't you get it?" I didn't wait for De's answer. I was psyched now. "The girl was made to be molded, shaped. It's fate, De." I tossed away the pillow and launched myself off the couch. "Sharon is the clay," I announced excitedly, "and I am the potter."

De's mouth flopped open.

"What?" I said. "Why are you staring at me like that?"

"Maybe," she began cautiously, "it's because I never heard you refer to yourself as a potty before."

"Potty!" I exclaimed as she slowly stood. "As if! I said potter. *Er*," I emphasized, following her out of the living room. "A potter is a person who works with clay," I persisted as De picked up speed heading for the door. "You know, making pots, or like little nut dishes, or those hand prints you talked about. It was just an analogy, I was simply pointing out the similarity between—"

"I know what an analogy is," De assured me, opening the front door. "And I know what a true-blue bud is, too."

"De, where are you going?" I asked as she bailed. "What did you want?"

She paused at the edge of the veranda. "Nothing as vital as playing with clay, Cher," she said coldly. "Only that the man I love seems to be phoning all my friends in search of hair pieces—but, of course, that's not as important as making a nut dish!"

"De, wait!" I protested. But she was gone. All that remained was the echo of her def pumps clacking across our circular driveway as she ran toward the street.

I was so bummed. I knew my girlfriend was in distress, yet I felt powerless to comfort her. A part of me wanted to dash after De and beg her forgiveness. But in our neighborhood walking is like a felony, let alone doing it barefoot in a smiley face nightie with unwashed hair. And also—and I am not saying that I'm proud of this—another part of me, I'd say at least fifty-five percent, felt viciously compelled to resume work on my project.

So I closed the door and slowly made my way upstairs again. By the time I chose three chronic ensembles for Sharon, then showered and changed—into this choice plum-toned sweater-and-leggings set from the Victoria's Secret catalog—Daddy and the step-gnome were home.

"Cher, we're ordering Chinese," Josh called up to me. "Want anything special?"

"An eggroll and some privacy," I responded, from the second floor landing. I was in one of my favorite positions: looking down on Josh. He, of course, was attired in his collegiate lumberjack best.

"Did you know that eggrolls are deep fried?" he asked, looking up at me with this smug little smile.

"Did you know that flannel is a clothing option, not a skin tone?" I snapped back.

When his grin disappeared, I took it as a victory. But the boy followed up with this deeply concerned "Cher, are you all right? You look exhausted."

"Thank you for your unsolicited opinion, Josh," I began. "You, of course, are an expert on—"

"Cher, what is this?" Daddy had suddenly appeared at Josh's side. He was clutching a yellow legal pad, from which he started reading. "Twenty-five to ninety percent of weight loss comes not from body fat but from muscles, organs, and fluids."

"You are absolutely the best, Daddy. I spent half the day looking for that pad," I said, hurrying down the stairs to retrieve it. "It's the fat-to-muscle makeover program I developed for Sharon."

"I could have read it aloud in court!" he said sharply.

"Sorry, Daddy. One of your legal dweebs must have picked it up by mistake yesterday and tucked it into your briefcase. But, whew, I'm so glad you found it," I told him. "I thought I'd have to prepare a whole new fitness plan."

"You don't look well," Daddy said, placing a paternal palm on my brow.

I ducked out from under his hand. "Well, duh. It must be this plum," I said, indicating the grape-stain shade of my viciously fresh mail-order outfit. "That's what I get for wearing winter when I am such a total spring. Really, I'm okay, Daddy."

"Did you tell Josh what you want for dinner?" he asked, still skeptically focused on me.

There were piles of publications strewn across my Laura Ashley bed quilt, back issues of *YM*, *Sassy*, *Sixteen*, *Seventeen*, *Allure*, *Vogue*, *Vibe*, and more. "Actually, I had a big lunch," I fibbed, wanting to get back upstairs. I was eager to complete the list of guy-getting techniques and dating tips I'd been putting together for Sharon. The advice columns of my fave 'zines were crammed with wisdom in this area.

"You've got to eat something besides an eggroll," Josh urged.

"Right, tell me about nourishment, you who think chocolate is a food group," I said. "I'll grab an apple if I'm starving, Daddy," I promised on my way up the stairs. "Don't worry about me. Just tell them not to put MSG, salt, or soy sauce on your order, okay? And no spare ribs."

Although I meant it, I also knew it was the surest way

to get Daddy off my case. He'll do anything to avoid nutrition discussions.

"But, Cher," my stepsib persisted.

Daddy grabbed his arm. "Leave her alone, Josh," he said. "Come on, we'll order on the phone in my office."

I hardly slept Saturday night. I had all these weird dreams. The only one I remembered was where I was telling Mom something about Sharon's makeover and I noticed this bitter lack of enthusiasm on her part. Then Josh, only dressed up from Victor Frankenstein's time, started telling Mom that I wasn't eating properly. And when I whirled around to tell him to mind his own business, he had turned into De. And she was saying that all Sharon really needed were hair extensions. Then she pulled on this lever and there was a crash of lightning, and next thing I knew, everyone was laughing at me. "You look just like Busta Rhymes," De was saying. And I could tell that my hair was brutally fried, all standing up in these electric dreads.

That was when I woke up. It was so fresh to find myself in a sunny room, with this gentle breeze from the ceiling fan stirring the air.

The red light on my answering machine was blinking proof of my popularity. I had not checked my messages since Friday. I got out of bed and into my pink bunny slippers. Dozens of publications, their vital pages flagged with pastel stickums, lay scattered across the plush carpeting. I pressed the button on my answering machine and began gathering up magazines as I listened to the familiar voices of yesterday's callers.

Lucas had checked in just to say hi. Sharon was confirming our twelve o'clock date with destiny. Murray was back with a plea for hair. Amber said there were still a few seats left at her cheer reading, but she couldn't guarantee me one.

And then there was Dionne. With a stack of *Sassy*s in my arms, I paused to hear her golden tones.

"Cher, it's ten A.M. You were supposed to call me back last night. Where are you?" There was urgency in her voice. "Girlfriend, I must speak with you." And then: "Cher, I'm worried sick. I've been dialing and paging you all morning. I'm coming over. And if you're not there and Lucy doesn't know where to find you, I'm taking it to nine-one-one." And, finally, after our encounter yesterday afternoon: "Cher, it's De. We have been best buds since grade school, and I feel it is my duty to say this. You are in the grip of a brutal obsession, girlfriend, and I am not talking Calvin Klein aromas here—"

"As if!" I cried aloud, and snapped off the machine. I had heard enough. I had a very busy day ahead of me. And only a few hours left to prepare for Sharon's arrival.

I set down the magazines in this neat pile and on my way into the bathroom checked out my hair in my dressing-table mirror. It was sleep ridden, sure. But it actually looked nothing like Busta Rhymes's shocked coif. My best friend had grievously exaggerated, both on the phone and in my dream.

Yet even as I flossed, I knew. I owed Dionne an apology. She had come to me in pain, and I had been too . . . preoccupied. Yes, that was it, I thought. Preoccupied. Not the psycho O word. I mean, obsessed is such a total ticket to the Jenny Jones show.

I resolved to phone Dionne and apologize for my preoccupation as soon as possible. But I had a million things to do before Sharon arrived at noon.

* * *

Time flew. Josh knocked on my door. "Sheee's bah-ack," he said in this dismal Schwarzenegger imitation. "That girl with the safety pin is waiting for you down-stairs."

"Already?" I asked, grabbing a peek at the 18K gold Longines with integrated bracelet on my wrist. It was precisely twelve o'clock. "I'm on my way," I said, gathering my notes. I heard Josh's footsteps descending the marble staircase. My hand was on the doorknob when I remembered my resolution and paused to speed dial De.

"Cher who?" Amber answered the phone.

"I don't even want to know why you're screening De's calls," I said. "Just put her on, Amber."

"What if she doesn't want to speak to you?" Amber asked.

"What if Mr. Hall compares the words to Tracy Chapman's 'Fast Car' with that poem you handed in for extra credit last week?"

"That is so petty," Amber grumbled.

Then I heard De in the background go, "It's okay. I'll talk to her." I waited. Finally, she got on and said in this seriously reserved voice, "Yes?"

"Oh, please, Dionne, not now," I urged. "You know I'm terrible at groveling. I just want to say that although I may not have behaved perfectly yesterday, I actually did hear your anguish and I was very moved by it."

"And?" said De.

"And, well, I haven't actually given all that much thought to why Murray wants secondhand hair, but I am with you in your struggle. I was way preoccupied yesterday. But I'll make it up to you any way I can."

"Ask if she'll lend you her red Alaïa with the marabou trim?" I heard Amber urging.

I was stunned. "Dionne, I can't believe you made me apologize on speakerphone," I gasped. "Who else is listening in on this, our entire class?"

"Not even!" De responded. "It's just Amber."

"What do you mean 'just'?" Amber loudly objected.

"Dionne, Sharon is downstairs right now. I've got to run. But don't worry about Murray, girlfriend. We'll get to the root of his hair fetish."

"Oh, Cher, do you think so?" she asked, a spark of hope lightening her tone.

"It's bitterly *X-Files*-esque. But, trust me, we'll work it out together," I promised. "Kiss, kiss, De. I'm bailing."

Reconnecting with my true blue was a furiously healing experience. I bounded downstairs, renewed, and found Sharon stretched out in the den. She was lying on the sofa, remote in hand, clicking through reruns on the tube. She barely acknowledged my entrance.

"Oh, hi." Making no effort to sit up, let alone stand, Sharon gazed at me. "You like *Road Rules?*" She indicated the MTV show she'd momentarily settled on.

"I'm usually way up and out at this hour," I responded. "So." I clapped my hands together in a show of energetic optimism. "Let's get started, shall we? Are you ready?"

Sluggishly, Sharon Clay struggled to her feet. "I guess," she murmured.

The following hours were spent in a whirlwind of improvement activities. I totally gave of myself, plying Sharon with dozens of extremely dope secrets, hints, clues, and pointers. We analyzed her colors, altered her clothing choices, reviewed nonmetallic accessories, experimented with subtle but effective makeup options, and critiqued basic fitness videos, choosing two excellent beginner tapes—a spin routine for aerobic exercise and this major abs punisher for toning.

At three-thirty, safety-pin free and wearing my pink terry robe, Sharon was seated before the mirror at my dressing table. Her hair, wrapped in a towel, was slick with time-released moisturizers delivering Vitamin E and rich emollients deep below the scalp surface. Waiting for the conditioner to revitalize her thirsty follicles, we began discussing dating procedures.

We'd gotten all the way to defensive flirting, when a knock at my door interrupted us. "Excuse me—what part of Do Not Disturb do you not understand?" I called irritably. "I am brutally busy here—"

The door flew open. It was Daddy. I was so startled. Usually, he dials me from downstairs or just hollers. "Oh, hi, Daddy," I said. "What are you doing up here?"

"What's wrong with your phone?" he wanted to know. He was leaning against the door jamb, panting slightly. Daddy is viciously out of shape. Yelling is his major cardiovascular workout.

"Nothing. I just turned it off," I said. "But it so busts fresh that you made the climb, Daddy. I was just telling Sharon—" I indicated my terrycloth-turbaned guest, who gave Daddy this unexpectedly all-out smile. I was totally kvelling. She was changing before my eyes, moving from sullenly apologetic to casually cheerful. Plus her teeth were way props. "—how effective it is to flirt with one boy in order to pique the interest of another," I finished.

Sharon asserted, "I would never do that, I can't."

"Sharon," I said delicately, "words like *can't* and *never* are not even in our personal dictionaries."

"Yes, well. Dionne is downstairs," Daddy announced.

My mouth fell open. "She knows how busy I am today. I mean, I am furiously in the midst of a major makeover and have zero time to even— Uh, how come you came up to tell me that, Daddy?"

"Because Dionne, Josh, and Lucy refused to interrupt you," he said. "Cher, what's going on here?"

I hurried to the door and gave Daddy this quick little peck on the cheek. "I'll explain everything later. Right now, Daddy, my humanitarian responsibilities demand full attention. Tell De I'll see her at school tomorrow," I said, giving him this teensiest hint of a shove. "I'm involved in transforming a tormented girl into a slammin' goddess, and I definitely sense victory ahead. Now, please, Daddy, just tell Sharon that triangular teasing is a fully effective tool for inciting jealousy. I mean, like if you like one boy, you make sure he catches you flirting with another, right?"

Daddy looked so cute and adorably confused. He scratched his head, which is regularly sheared by a close friend of Kevyn Aucoin who makes house calls in the Beverly Hills area and carries his blow dryer in this def leather holster. "Whatever," he mumbled supportively.

I closed the door and resumed work.

Dionne did not go home. As I later learned, she and Josh spent the afternoon sipping caffeine-free soft drinks and doggin' on me. De had asked Josh whether he'd noticed my growing similarity to a certain tormented Mary Shelley character.

Josh affirmed that he had. Brow bogusly scrunched with worry, he'd cited my goal to singlehandedly improve my species.

"Tscha!" Dionne had agreed. And what about the way I was avoiding friends, working in this frenzy of ambition, and growing not merely pale but, my personal favorite, feverishly obsessed.

I learned all this from my good friend Lucy, who supplied bowls of popcorn and taco chips to the analysts of my personal McLaughlin Group. Lucy traded me the information for a written promise to call the contractor and schedule a kitchen renovation.

But I didn't know this at five P.M., when Sharon and I emerged from my room. As we walked down the stairs together, Josh and De came out of the den and stood gaping up at us.

Moisture rich, Sharon's squeaky clean hair flowed goldenly onto her proudly erect shoulders. The champagne blond shade we'd settled on excellently accented her tiger-bright eyes. Actually, her whole face was bathed in a healthy glow, achieved through the expert application of quality makeup products.

I had lent her this adorable faux leopard miniskirt and skinny black velour top. They so went with my new midcalf boots, which were only like a half size too small for her.

I was so proud.

Of course, carrying a shopping bag full of Sharon's garmental discards, including her hefty chain-link accessories and scuffed, steel-toed boots, and like pounds of self-help books and magazines, I myself was slightly stooped. Plus, I had hardly slept or eaten in days.

"I'm majorly wiggin'," Dionne shrieked, staring at me. "I totally cannot believe my eyes. Sharon, you look so . . . different!"

"Hello." I tried to contain my annoyance. "That's because I'm not Sharon," I corrected my hyper bud.

"Cher?" Dionne gasped.

"Bingo," I said, handing Sharon the heavy bag. "Well,

I think we can say this makeover is a brilliant success," I told my client. "Especially since no one here even recognizes you."

"Sharon?" De and Josh gasped at once.

"Totally," the renovated girl gushed. "So, Cher. What are you wearing to school tomorrow?"

I put my arm through hers, and we swept past Josh and De. "I'm thinking my quilted chartreuse Chanel suit. It's frantically hot off the rack with black piping. And with my polyamide and elastin body suit by Jil Sander, it seriously burns."

"Hoops or danglies?" Sharon asked, fingering her bare earlobes.

"Teardrops, mock pearl, I think," I said, giving her arm an encouraging squeeze.

"Chronic choice," she agreed. "With flats, stiletto heels, or stacks?"

"Black stack-heel loafers by Nine West."

"Jammin'," said Sharon. She waved goodbye to Dionne and Josh, then turned to me, and, puckering her pale pink glossed lips, went, "Okay, kiss, kiss."

Chapter 7

*H*i, Cher," I heard someone shout. "That ensemble is way Evangelista. Major snaps."

It was Monday morning. De and I were ambling across campus, trying to decipher Murray's hair mania. As always, our classward stroll had been repeatedly interrupted by fans calling out to us.

I cheerfully turned to acknowledge the greeting. But there was no one with whom to make eye contact. Shrugging, I returned to our conversation. "I think freaking is way premature here, De," I said. "So let's ponder. Why would Murray be collecting hair specimens?"

"Worst case scenario?" De speculated. "Because he's fallen for someone new."

"Not even! Like he's smitten with some folliclely challenged graduate of the Sinead O'Connor school of beauty? I don't think so," I said.

"She wouldn't have to be bald," De begged to differ.

A random high school boy in a backward cap screeched to a halt beside us. His rubber-soled Kanis left tread burns on the grass. "Cher, whassup? Wasn't you just inhaling a croissant at the joe bar in the Quad?"

"Excuse me?" I said to the starstruck teen. "I'm afraid you're mistaken."

"Naw, naw, naw." The boy shook his head in vigorous disagreement. "You were there. You were wearing that same puffy green suit with the black outline."

"Puffy? Hello. It is quilted." I tried to maintain a polite smile. "And it is so not green. It's chartreuse. And what you call outlined, fashion cognoscenti know as piping. Now, if you'll excuse us?"

He backed off, and I took De's arm. "So, you really think Murray's scoring swatches for a new love?" I resumed.

"Well, I don't know." De batted her hazel eyes helplessly. "If there's not another woman involved, then what?"

"Then lots of stuff," I said. "I mean, for all we know, Murray is collecting hair specimens for some charity project."

"Please. Like Hair for the Homeless would be such a worthy cause."

"Well, it would," I protested. "Everyone has a right to look decent. De, I bet it's got something to do with the Monster Bash. You should definitely confront him. Like just ask why."

She shook her head adamantly, setting in motion the cluster of lustrous curls piled on top of her head and bound by these choice baby blue ribbons. "I promised to cease and desist all confrontations with my man, at least until after the Bash," she reminded me. "Plus, I'm bitterly vulnerable right now. It's the trust issue. Murray would think I doubted him."

"Which you do," I pointed out.

"Yes, but I don't have to prove that he's right. And, anyway, it's like your father always says, never ask a question you don't already have the answer to."

"Cher, Cher! Wait up!" Once more I turned, prepared to acknowledge my popularity with a wave and a wink.

My raised hand froze in midair. My fingers wilted into these total talons. I gasped.

"What's wrong?" De shouted, protectively clutching me. Then, turning to see what I'd seen, she shrieked aloud.

There I was. I mean, there I was coming toward me. A mirror image of my once distinctive self was rushing across the Quad, pausing only briefly to return a wave, a wink, or a blown kiss from an adoring fan.

"Cher," the girl said breathlessly, pulling alongside De and me.

"Sharon?" De and I screeched together.

"Totally," Sharon asserted. "How awesome am I? Everyone's been complimenting me on this suit, which my mom's seamstress totally whipped up last night."

"An excellent replica," I had to admit.

"And did she like 'whip up' those pearl teardrops, too?" De demanded.

Sharon tossed back her gleaming mane of golden hair to better reveal the earrings on which De had fixated. "They're just like Cher's," the former grunge goddess gushed, "only faux, of course."

"'Faux' is so the operative term here," De grumbled, eyeing my fashion twin.

"Of course it's faux," I agreed. "There's only one me."

But, De, you have to admit, in terms of makeovers, this may be my ultimate triumph."

I was circling Sharon, studying her apparel, posture, hairstyle, and makeup. Even more impressive was the new confidence and sunny disposition my star pupil was displaying.

"Were you over at the school joe bar a few minutes ago?" De quizzed the girl.

"Totally!" she replied with vicious perkiness. "I was waiting for Cher at your reserved table and this guy Miles brought me a cup of cappuccino—"

"Liberally dusted with cinnamon," said De.

"Totally," Sharon agreed. "And this crusty croissant. So I just sat there and was like nibbling and waiting, and everyone kept coming up and saying these totally excellent things about me."

The shock of seeing myself replicated, however imperfectly, was wearing off. A soaring sense of achievement replaced my last misgivings. Never had anyone so quickly absorbed and adapted my wit and wisdom.

"And then your friend Amber plopped herself down next to me," Sharon continued, "and like kept asking if I was going to eat the rest of my croissant. And I was all, 'Yes, totally,' and she started going, 'Oh, I thought you were so allergic to high-cal pastries. And like you'd never eat anything with over two grams of fat in it.' And 'Are you sure you want the other half?'"

"Amber thought you were Cher," De marveled.

"Did you give her the croissant?" I asked.

"Not even," she asserted.

"Yessss!" I cheered, punching the air. I stepped back and took her hands. "Sharon," I said, misty eyed, "you are a furiously viable Betty, poised at the brink of a frantic popularity breakthrough."

"Yesss!" she agreed, breaking free of my grasp, her fist puncturing the smog-thickened L.A. sky.

"Cher, you can't be serious," Dionne said, comparing my attire with Sharon's nearly identical ensemble. "You went bitterly postal when Amber wore the same scarf as you to that low party in the Valley."

"As Emilio Estevez would say, 'That was then, this is now,'" I told my disbelieving bud. "Anyway, imitation is the sincerest form of flattery. Right, Sharon?"

Her excellently accented tiger eyes flashed. "Totally," she agreed.

I was so exhilarated. All morning long, I witnessed my peer group's stunned reactions to my most stellar makeover ever. It was easy because Sharon never left my side. Not even when her class schedule brutally differed from mine, like starting with first period, when I had social studies and she was slated for P.E.

After De left us, we ran into Tai in the corridor on the way to Ms. Geist's class. She was wearing these monster designer shades, and she totally freaked when she saw us. "You are a full-out miracle worker, Cher," she announced.

I basked in her praise, until I noticed that she was facing Sharon. "Over here, Tai." I waved my hand at her face. "Those are chronic Armanis, girlfriend, but way dark for bud sightings."

"Way dark but furiously chronic," Sharon agreed.

I smiled at her supportively as Tai ambled off. "Well, I'm history," I said, preparing to slip into social studies. "See you later, Sharon."

"I don't think so." Those gold-flecked eyes held mine insistently. "The fate of our nation is way meaningful to me," she recited, "so, I thought I'd just sit in on Geist's class with you."

"That is so commendable, but—" I began.

"I mean, didn't you brutally lecture me on the importance of do-goodism and social responsibility?" she queried. "And isn't social studies the total cradle of all that stuff, putting, as it does, current events into a historical perspective?"

"You're anxious about going to gym, right?" I asked delicately. "I mean like about getting all smelly and sweated up and having your hair and makeup go disastrously bad?"

"Whatever," she conceded.

"Okay." I patted her hand. "Just for today."

As we entered the classroom, Ryder Hubbard, the burnt-out boardie, did this overly dramatic double take. "Whew, dudes, I'm having an *It Takes Two* moment," he announced, scratching his scraggly chin hairs. "Like, which one of you is Mary-Kate and which one is Ashley?"

Sharon bristled defensively. But I arched an eyebrow at the slacker, opting to tame him with attitude. "The Olsen twins. Duh, why am I not impressed? That reference is bitterly ripe, Ryder," I noted. "When dropping names, you generally want to go for celebs over four feet tall."

"Except for like Danny DeVito," Sharon mused. "But trying to like impress someone by mentioning the Olsen twins—duh, that is totally ripe."

"Sharon?" Olivia Ackst, a finger in her nostril, looked up from fastening her nose ring and stared at us as we moved along the aisle to find seats. "Wow, you look . . . weird," she said. "What did you do to your hair, wash it or what?"

"And you are?" Sharon shot her former bud a full-out cold front and moved on.

"Oh, excuse me," Olivia called after us, giving her two-toned head a haughty shake. "I didn't know you were in with the in crowd now, bouncing with the Bettys, hangin' with the Galleria gang."

Our double Chanels confused Ms. Geist at first, but basically she had no problem with my protégé sitting in. Without the safety pin to clue her, Geist just assumed Sharon was a new girl who hadn't gotten her schedule yet. We had similar success in all my classes and caused a vicious stir wherever we went, especially in the hallways. Everyone was like, Whoops, how double am I seeing? It was all, "Two! Two! Two Chers in one!"

Sharon clung to me like Velcro. She was a monster mimic, brutally attuned to my every word and gesture. Yet, I have to say that after a while, it did sort of blow knowing that whatever I said, I'd instantly hear again—with totally thrown in like this personal flourish on a counterfeit signature.

Still, I was upbeat. All morning, kids whirled around to stare at us. Mouths, carefully outlined in beige tones, gaped speechlessly. Behind tinted designer lenses, eyes blinked in disbelief. Until, at last, it was lunchtime.

"Just wave and smile and don't do autographs now 'cause it'll eat into our munch break," I advised Sharon as I snapped open my phone and dialed De.

"Let's rendezvous outside Hanratty's class, girlfriend," I cellularly suggested. "Refreshments Quadside in five. Sharon and I are doing a triumphal march past the junior lockers. We'll be swinging over to math right about—"

"Now," De finished the sentence, joining us, cell phone still at her ear.

"What a morning. I'm brutally kvelling," I said, snapping shut my phone.

"Me, too," Sharon confided. "Totally kuh-velling."

"It's *kvelling*," De corrected her. "The word has only two syllables. And do you even know what it means?"

"Duh. No," Sharon went, putting her index finger to her temple in a gesture so familiar to me. "But Cher says it all the time."

"It means like being proud and thrilled—" I started to explain as we left the corridor din for the blinding sunlight and manicured Astroturf of the Alcott campus.

"Proud and thrilled." Sharon abruptly cut me off. "And I so am!" she declared, turning to acknowledge a gaping gang of ninth-grade girls.

De arched an eyebrow at me. "This is your doing, girlfriend," she muttered.

"What are you talking about?" I asked as the gaggle of admirers approached us, giggling excitedly. I turned, prepared to sign an autograph or two.

But they circled Sharon like a crew of baby piranhas. "I remember when you used to wear that safety pin," one of them gushed worshipfully. It was like she was reminding Madonna of her pre-*Evita* bustier period. Not one of the pubescent posse paid homage to Dionne or me.

"You've created a monster," said De.

"You are so wrong," I countered. "I took a total Janeane Garofalo and turned her into a brutal Uma. Survey says," I insisted, "she is my greatest success."

"What are we having for lunch?" Sharon asked me as we moved along the cafeteria line.

"I ate like a heifer this morning, an entire English muffin. So, I'm thinking greens. No dressing. Hold the bacon bits and croutons," I said. "And like maybe a frozen yogurt for dessert. The raspberry is notorious. Only one gram of fat."

"Frozen yogurt. That's totally what I'm thinking," Sharon confessed.

"Uncanny coincidence," De murmured sarcastically, then busied herself picking avocado chunks out of the sushi roll she'd snagged.

"You're not throwing those away?" Amber, in a blindingly garish yellow and black checked pants suit, was pushing through the line toward us. "Excuse me, want to suck in the abs, please, I can't get through. Excuse me, wicked hat, saw it on Rodeo—in a donation bin. Seriously, Dionne," she said, having reached us, "you're not going to trash those avocados, are you?"

"Why would I do that," De asked, checking out Amber's rancid ensemble, "when I could get a tax write-off donating them to the starving fashion victims of Brentwood?"

As De forked over her calorie-laden avocado discards, Amber's evil gaze took in Sharon and me. "Tell me about fashion," she drawled. "At least Mary-Kate and Ashley don't do identical off-the-racks."

"That reference is bitterly ripe, Amber," Sharon declared. "I mean like when dropping names, you generally want to go for celebs over four feet tall. Right, Cher?"

"Totally," I said.

De examined Sharon with new respect. "That was a way decent rejoinder," she decided.

Even Amber gave the girl a reluctant thumbs-up. "It didn't fully suck," she admitted.

We moved into the dessert sector. De was torn between an apricot mousse from Spago and Martha

Stewart's country-style rice pudding. It was a demanding choice and she was frowning. Suddenly, her concentration gave way to a mischievous grin. "Look who's coming." She elbowed me. "Every hockey fan's favorite July."

"Is Lucas here?" I asked, craning to catch a glimpse of my Baldwin.

"Over there, near Raphael," De said.

"Where?" Sharon gripped the throttle of the frozen yogurt dispenser so hard that her knuckles whitened.

"He's weaving through the outcast section, being nice to dorks, stooges, slackers, and nerds," Amber said. "Okay, now he's heading this way."

The moment I caught sight of my man, it was as though a thousand points of light suddenly warmed my heart——like when everyone does the candle thing at the end of a concert. It was a brutal metabolic rush. My pulse was so pumped, I could have worked off a burger just staring at him.

Lucas was wearing his hockey jersey, with an excellent pair of preshrunk, stone-washed Eddie Bauers. His broad shoulders moved nimbly with every athletically correct step he took. He was, as Amber had pointed out, stopping to chat with a vast assortment of cafeteria types, not just his calendar constituency.

"I still don't see him." Sharon scanned the lunchroom.

"Over there." I pointed him out discreetly. "See, there's Raphael, and Lucas is right behind him."

Blotches bloomed on Sharon's face, but she quickly returned to her task, which was to plunge down the dispenser handle and release a thick, curling stream of raspberry frozen yogurt into one of Bronson Alcott's fluted crystal ice cream bowls.

I raised my hand to signal Lucas. But suddenly, Raphael was standing in front of me, his tall, rangy bod totally blocking my hottie-viewing space.

"Princess," he said exuberantly, "missed you this morning. Way too much happening for a Monday. My cleaning at the periodontist ran into overtime, so I missed Hall's class. Then my dad's Ferrari went berserko and I had to take it into the shop. I would have called them to pick it up, only I was so not supposed to be cruising in it—"

I tried to peek around Raphael's leather-clad shoulders to catch a glimpse of Lucas, but the agitated new boy was explaining his morning bummer with flailing hand signals and full body descriptives.

"I'm on a learner's permit till spring," he continued. "But I borrowed Dad's wheels, thinking maybe I'd run into you above Sunset and give you a lift. But after the dental delay, I must have clicked in the wrong key code on the mighty Ferrari. So I'm sitting at Doheny with lights and horns and bells blaring. And nothing to see me through but the thought of you." Suddenly, Raphael seized my hand and pressed it to his lips again.

I tore it from his grasp and actually shoved him aside. But it was too late. There was Lucas, his mouth flopped open. I could tell by his expression that he'd caught me—not red handed but definitely wet knuckled. Clearly, he had witnessed Raphael's second impetuous kiss.

"Hi, Lucas," I called. But suddenly, Sharon's hand—the one I'd personally reconstituted with moisturizers and manicuring tips—reached up and touched my blond hottie's stylishly stubbly cheek. I gasped as Sharon turned Lucas's head away from me.

"This frozen yogurt is excellent, Lucas," she announced loudly enough for Raphael to turn and stare, too. "The raspberry is totally notorious. Only one gram of fat."

I gaped, astonished, as the Betty I'd created spooned a curl of frozen raspberry yogurt into the startled mouth of my calendar hunk.

I couldn't believe my fresh blue eyes. Sharon, who had been grievously incapable of making even a dessert choice, had suddenly gone independent—and was flirting with my man.

"Do I know you?" Raphael quizzed the girl.

"As if!" Sharon retorted. As he stared at her, scratching his head, she turned abruptly, handed Lucas her tray, and with a "Kiss, kiss, catch you guys later," she whisked my honey away.

Stunned, like a deer staring at the headlights of an oncoming car or me missing an unannounced sale at Prada, I watched them hurry off. I could feel the love candles in my heart go out one by one. An icky chill set in.

One minute I'd been proudly nurturing my protégée and looking forward to a snuggly encounter with my fave uomo. The next, Raphael was in my face, and Sharon and Lucas were history. Hello, this was so not the scheduled scenario.

"Raphael, could you excuse us, please," I managed to say. "I'd like a private moment with my friends."

"No problem," the dark-haired knuckle sucker said. "Even this brief encounter with you has brightened my formerly bogus day."

He reached for my hand again, but I whisked it away and waggled my fingers. "Hasta la vista," I said.

"Terminator II." He made the connection. "Arnold says it right before he blows someone away."

"I think you'd better bail," De suggested, and he did.

But even before Raph grabbed a Cobb salad and sauntered, the colorful cafeteria din seemed to dull around me. The clatter of dishes and trays, the steamy shush of the cappuccino machine, students calling to one another, trading secrets, trashing teachers, laughing and then like choking, and spewing refreshments out of their noses—everything paled to a low, gray rumble. My Technicolor world seemed totally washed out.

"Cher?" De's voice was gentle. "Are you all right?"

Amber's cosmetically overassisted eyes widened. "Hello. Will someone please tell me what is going on?" she sang.

"Do something different, Amber," De advised, wrapping a slender arm around my Chanel-quilted shoulder. "Try keeping at least one of those size nines out of your mouth."

Although I knew De was trying to be supportive, I sensed a soupçon of pity in her comforting gesture. It brought me rudely to my senses. What was I torn up about anyway? Hadn't Sharon simply been following flirting instructions, and doing a massively def job at it. I should totally be plotzing with pride, not grieving the unlikely loss of my favorite senior. Get over it, Cher, I called myself back from bummer land. Which is so not a place I care to dwell.

"How choice was that?" Focusing on the most positive aspects of the recent debacle, I shrugged off De's arm, placed my empty food tray on the rack beside the salad bar, and started for the patio. "Coming?" I asked my startled buds.

"Choice?" After a moment's hesitation, Dionne caught up with me. Amber snagged a bunch of grapes off a cottage cheese and fruit plate and hurried after us.

"Sharon Clay, the revised edition," I continued, by-passing our reserved table with a carefree wave to Tai and Baez, "has just successfully completed one of the most difficult makeover moves a candidate can master."

"What's that, brutally humiliating and betraying a friend?" Amber asked. Then, responding to De's icy glare, she rolled her eyes and added, "Well, excuse me."

"In case you didn't notice, Amber, the formerly tongue-tied teen castoff has just successfully chatted up Bronson Alcott's most Baldwinian babe," I explained, leading my t.b.'s to one of my favorite meditation haunts on campus, the bleachers overlooking the sports fields. I needed to relax, loosen up. For some reason, my chakras felt furiously unaligned. "A maneuver," I pointed out, "that she could so not have mastered without my help."

"And what?" Amber demanded, scampering up the bleachers behind De and me. "That's golden?"

"As golden as my hottie's clean locks," I asserted. "It totally affirms my triumph as a makeover mentor."

I plunked myself down and stared out at the playing fields. On the baseball diamond, some kids were unen-thusiastically lobbing a ball around. Likewise in the volleyball sand pits. And yet again on the tennis courts. I tried to get into the hypnotic rhythms of the listless thwacks and thumps and just go with the flow. Bore-dom is like the essence of meditation.

De sat beside me. "Well, if it's a triumph," she said, just as I was starting to feel way lulled, "then I say it calls for a monster mall hit. We can celebrate your unprece-dented achievement. And Sharon's graduation from clueless to clone."

"Mega scheme, De. Major snaps." I was suddenly

stoked. "Galleria at three," I affirmed. "Available credit status?"

We pulled out our organizers. "Let's see. I've got enough left on my Gold card to storm at least three upscale national chains," De announced, "and finance a furious food court pig out."

"Cheese nachos." Amber wrinkled her surgically enhanced nose, then laughed. "I'm in."

"Après school, then," I summarized. And we bounded down the bleachers and across the Quad, bursting through the bronze doors of the main building moments before the class bell sounded.

Chapter 8

Why did you even bring her?" Dionne asked me. We were at the mall. Sharon had taken a rest room detour, and laden with shopping bags, De, Amber, and I were waiting for her outside Express.

"Because she asked what we were doing, Dionne. What was I supposed to say?"

"You could have tried, 'Nothing to which you are invited,' " Amber suggested helpfully.

My buds had appeared surprised, but nevertheless had behaved graciously when I met them outside school with Sharon at my side—which was where she'd been all afternoon. "She was waiting for me in algebra, after lunch," I told them now, "all excited because guess where she went with Lucas?"

"I'm not sure I want to know," De said, tightening one of the slender blue ribbons wrapped around her curls. It had come loose during our fitting room spree.

Over the head try-ons are lethal 'do destroyers. But De's repairs were well under way.

"To the office to change her schedule! In addition to officially trying to transfer into all my classes, Sharon followed me throughout the afternoon," I confided. "The girl desperately depends on me. She turns to me for the answers to all questions, solicits my opinion in controversial matters, likes what I like, hates what I hate. I'm frantically exhausted. It's like I'm living a double life, my own and hers. She totally worships me."

"Did I miss anything?" Sharon was back.

"Just the outer corner of your lid where the liner doesn't go all the way across," Amber said. "So, is it nachos and cheese time? Are we starving?"

"Are we?" Sharon turned to me.

"Hello," said De. "This is a group decision based on individual inclinations. In other words, Sharon, are *you* ripe for a gorge?"

"I am," I responded.

"Famished," Sharon said.

The food court was rampant with random types. A Benetton array of high school homeys in oversize team jackets by Perry Ellis and Tommy Hilfiger stalked the aisles with trays of pizza, doughnuts, and bogus Chinese food in their hands. Dysfunctional family pageants were taking place at every other table. Lerner's-size moms were force-feeding their young on huge salted pretzels and greasy fries. Here and there, the stylish lapped frozen yogurts and stole jealous glances around them, coveting their neighbor's nachos.

Amber led us through the lively scene to a nearly clean table for four. "Hello, you with the service cart." She signaled a bus person.

"Anyone want to split an order of curly fries with

me?" De queried as the not altogether unattractive boy Amber had summoned tidied our table with a grungy rag.

"I will," I said.

"Me, too," said Sharon.

"Sorry, Sharon." De shook her head. "Three on an order is too many. That would be like five fries apiece. It's hardly worth the grease gain."

"Oh, really," Sharon said curtly. But Amber perked up, prepared to negotiate.

"I'm doing nachos and melted cheese," she announced. "So, if you get curly fries, Sharon, we can split them both."

Sharon glanced my way. I nodded. She said, "Okay." And then she added, "By the way, Amber, call me Shar, okay?"

There was a moment of silence at our table. You could have heard a hem drop. "Cher?" Amber repeated cautiously.

De and I looked at each other. "Did she say 'Cher'?" De inquired.

"Duh, no," Sharon insisted. "Not Cher. *Shar*. You know, like for short."

The subtle difference was so lost on me. Dionne leaped to her feet. "Excuse me, please. Cher—" Carefully pronouncing my name, she grabbed my wrist. "Come on. I'll get the drinks, you pick up the fries."

Amber stood abruptly. "And I'll snag the nachos."

Sharon started to get up. "No." Amber put a restraining hand on her shoulder. "You stay here and save the table, okay, uhm, *Shar*?"

"Stay," I commanded. "Sit. We'll be right back."

"Yes. Stay." Mindlessly, De gave the hand signal she'd learned in puppy training class. Then, with Amber close behind us, she swept me away from the table and practically dragged me over to the fast food stalls.

With my back against the burgers and fries counter, my buds flanked me for a heart to heart. I listened, although it was hard to concentrate with the seductive stench of charred cow in my nostrils. But I heard enough to understand that my best friends were urging me to cut the girl loose.

"How can I?" I cried. "I created her. Now she won't associate with Olivia or any of the few friends she had before. They're heinously envious of her. She'd be so alone without me."

"Cher, I hate to bring this up again, but let's examine the scenario through, say, Mary Shelley's eyes," De suggested. "With awesomely excellent intentions, you set out to create a superior being. And much to everyone's surprise, you massively improved the girl's looks, zapping exciting new life into a formerly forlorn grunge queen. Yet what happened?"

"Yuck, she's turned into a Velcro body suit," Amber insisted.

"I don't always agree wholeheartedly with Amber," De interjected, "but in this, we are one. Plus, this new Sharon has vicious manhunter tendencies. Recall her ill-conceived play for Lucas just hours ago."

"Lucas was miffed at me because of Raphael's rash kiss," I began dismissively. And then it came to me. Right there, with burger flames lapping at my back and vapors of bubbling fat mingling with the fresh shampoo and just a scooch of environmentally correct nonaerosol holding mist in my hair, I remembered what Frankenstein's monster had really wanted. "De," I yelped, "he wanted a mate. That's all he wanted."

"Who, Lucas or Raphael?" she asked.

"No, the monster," I cried.

"Oh, you mean Sharon?" said De.

"That's way harsh," Amber scolded us. "I don't want to call her Shar either, but monster is a massive diss."

I glanced over at the table. Sharon was waiting for us. She looked bitterly chronic. Her makeup was subtle, flattering her naturally pale skin and wickedly prominent cheekbones. The Chanel suit fit her like a quilted glove, and she was not marring its fine lines by slumping. I was surprised at how my heart swelled at the sight of her. She was paging through a brochure on skin care that we'd picked up at the Clinique counter. It was a seriously informative piece, yet I doubted it would occupy her for long.

"Dionne, I'm having a total brainstorm. Remember how lonely the creature was and how he begged Frankenstein for a companion? Maybe if Vic had kept his promise and created a decent partner, the monster wouldn't have gone postal on him."

"And followed him everywhere." De instantly recognized the parallels. "Not just to Hanratty's, Geist's, and Hall's classes, but clear up to the North Pole."

"Hello," Amber practically shouted. "Will someone fill me in? I'm having an English-as-a-second-language moment."

I knew Amber's frustration, yet time was running out. "In essence, Amber," I said, cutting to the chase, "I'm going to sacrifice my own well-being to aid my protégée. I'm going to fix Sharon up with Lucas for the Bash."

"Not even!" Dionne shouted. Half the food court turned to stare. She lowered her voice. "Don't do it, girlfriend. Think it through. This is so not the only and seriously not the best solution."

"Well, it is what Sharon needs," I decided, "a buff companion, a decent date."

"What Sharon needs is half an order of cheese nachos," Amber said, and strode off toward the appropriate stall, her yellow-and-black ensemble giving new meaning to the phrase "making a beeline."

"Can I talk you out of this folly?" De asked as I turned to put in our curly fries order.

"No more than Henry Clerval could talk Victor out of his inspired project," I confessed. "An order of curly fries, please," I told the counterman. "And if you haven't got safflower oil, which is one of our healthier fats, then could you please use like a canola-based product? And we'd like the fries medium, you know, not burnt but darker than beige, and blotted on a clean paper towel. Thanks."

"But why Lucas?" De wanted to know.

"Because he appears to be her Baldwin of choice. I mean, didn't Amber overhear Sharon telling Lucas that she had a thing for a guy who was flipped over me? And anyway, De, it's just for the dance. Everyone will see her with Alcott's finest. It'll give her esteem a brutal boost."

"Oh, no!" De cried.

"Yes, it will," I insisted. "It will definitely—"

"Over there." De's classic hazel eyes were buggin' with distress. "It's Murray—with Kimberly Woo!"

I scanned the food court, trying to follow her gaze. There they were: Dionne's own Murray, presenting the raven-haired Kimberly with a monster, mustard-slathered pretzel.

"You have got to confront him, De. Go on over," I prodded.

"I will," Dionne asserted. She grabbed this big yellow-

and-red pamphlet from the burgers and fries counter and headed off in Murray and Kimberly's direction.

"You go, girl!" I cheered her on in *Waiting to Exhale*-speak, which was one of the freshest movies ever made on the theme of All Men Are Dogs. As she careered through the food court, I had a moment of apprehension about how De intended to use the handbill she'd snagged. Was my outraged bud going to roll up the leaflet and use it to beat her main boo senseless—which, seeing that he'd appeared in public with Kimberly at a Galleria we regularly visit, seemed redundant.

But as she neared the clueless couple, it became clear that De was not in Angela Bassett mode. She snapped open the oversize pamphlet and stuck her nose in it. Pretending to be deeply absorbed in its contents, she hurried past Murray and Kimberly, out of the food court, and back into the heavily trafficked mall.

Troubled, I picked up our curly fries and made my way to the table where Sharon and Amber were waiting. Amber's brow was furrowed as she concentrated on dividing the nachos into two even helpings. "What happened to De?" she asked.

My cell phone rang. "That's probably her now," I said. Setting down the fries, I pulled my Motorola out of my backpack and clicked on.

"Cher?" Dionne said in a frantic whisper.

"Girlfriend, where are you?" I asked as Amber's hand, quick as a lizard's tongue, snagged two of my curly fries.

"Don't look, don't look. I'm behind the Your-Photo-on-a-T-Shirt cart," De hissed, "where these three generations are bickering over the right computer image for an I-Love-Grandma dishtowel and brutally obstructing my view. Did they see me?"

"Murray and Kimberly? I don't think so." I peered across the room at them. "No, they're like all involved."

I heard De gasp. "Let me rephrase that," I quickly amended. "They're talking, and he's like showing her something in a book."

"A book?" De said frantically. "What do you mean, a book?"

"A book, Dionne. Your basic portable, rectangular object teeming with pages. The very reading material on which many of our favorite movies, TV miniseries, and spoken word audiotapes are based."

"Is it a little book?" she wailed. "You know, a slender volume type. The kind that lame inspirational sayings and love poems come in?"

"I can't tell from here," I said.

"Duh. Then go look, Cher. Hurry up," she urged.

"Dionne, does the Your-Photo cart have paper bags?" I asked.

"No, but the crystals and hair accessories cart does—"

Dionne was brutally hyperventilating. "Girlfriend," I said, gently but firmly, "go get a bag. Right now, De."

I grabbed a curly fry while I held on. I could hear De negotiating with the crystals and hair accessories people. "Okay, I'll buy something," she whimpered. "Here's my Visa. Give me that tiny glass horse with the horn on his head. Okay, the crystal unicorn for healing and hope. Just put it in a paper bag. Thank you so much. Got it, Cher," she said breathlessly.

"Okay, now. Put the bag over your nose. Blow out. Breathe in."

"Ouch!" De yelped.

"You didn't take out the unicorn, right?"

"You didn't tell me to, did you?" De said irritably.

"I'm lucky I don't have a unicorn lodged in my nostril. I think my nose is bleeding. I am so over this. I'm bailing before Murray sees me and launches into yet another dramatic you-don't-trust-me lecture."

"Excellent idea," I said.

"And you'll reveal yourself to him, check out the book, and get back to me," De instructed. "And don't forget my shopping bags and the three-for-the-price-of-two earrings I went in on with Amber. They're in her bag. Mine are the dangly prisms."

"Go home, De," I urged her, "and take care of that nose."

Daddy and Josh were just sitting down to dinner when I got in. My arms were loaded down with packages and shopping bags, but I rushed right into the dining room.

"Sorry I'm late," I said, leaning over to kiss Daddy's head and casually inspect his scalp for results of the follicle-replenishing treatment I'd talked him into using.

"Where have you been?" Daddy demanded, ducking his head and playfully batting away my probing fingers. "How much did you spend, young lady? And who is Lucas?"

"Let me take a stab at that first question," Josh said, with an amused smirk. "Was it the library? An art museum or concert? Or the mall?"

"Oh, like multiple choice is so hard," I responded. "Anyway, Daddy"—I indicated the parcels I was still holding—"these are not all mine. Like only two of them and the four shoe boxes are. The rest are De's. So really I saved you lots of money today. Which, by the way, we'll need for the rest of the kitchen renovations." I just threw that in quickly and moved on. "So did Lucas call?"

"Three times," he said. "Who is this guy?"

"Only one of the most popular people in the senior class," I replied.

Daddy lowered his head and studied me over the rims of his reading glasses. "A senior. I assume he drives, then."

"A brutally noble Porsche." Daddy is ferociously negative about teen drivers, which is way unfair, since practically the only one he's driven with is me.

"And what is he to you?"

"Lucas is my date for the Monster Bash, Daddy," I said, "one of the most fun fiestas of the school year. Only I'm going to fix him up with this needy protégée of mine. Her name is Sharon, and she needs a date much more than I do," I continued, avoiding Josh's judgmental gaze. "So don't give it another thought, Daddy. You probably won't even have to meet him for a while, let alone prepare a threatening fatherly talk to terrorize him. Unless he comes over tonight, because, frankly, Daddy, I think the ambiance here is so much better than at school for what I have to discuss with Lucas. So I'll just go call him and be right back."

"Sit down," Daddy barked.

"Daddy, I have to at least wash my hands. I've been shopping," I reminded him. "And I'm not talking Rodeo Drive. We were at the Galleria, a majorly public mall, where you have no way of knowing who handled the Calvins and DKNYs before you."

"Go, go." Daddy waved me away.

I dropped my packages onto the raw silk settee in the entry hall, gave Mom's portrait a quick wink, and hurried into the powder room. Turning on the taps full blast for sound effects, I dialed Lucas's cell phone. As water spewed from the mouth of our adorable gold dolphin faucet into the marble seashell-shaped sink, I waited. Finally, my honey picked up.

"Hi, Lucas, it's Cher," I crooned. "My dad says you phoned."

"Yeah, three times." There was a hint of upset in his normally mellow tone. Was he nurturing a resentment over the Raphael episode? I wondered. But then he went, "I don't know how to say this, Cher, but is your family in the witness protection program or something? That guy who answered your phone was seriously harsh. He asked me a lot of questions, some of them pretty personal, too. And when I admitted I had a date with you, he wanted to know if I'd ever seen this movie, *The Godfather,* and did my dad own a horse. Is he like a bodyguard or what?"

"As if!" I said indignantly. "That was just Daddy. He's a litigator. They're the most vicious lawyers there are. Sometimes he takes his work home with him." I heard traffic noises. "So where are you?" I asked.

"On my way home."

"Which one?" Lucas lives with his mom in Brentwood most of the time, but his dad has this twelve-room beach cottage in the Colony and his stepdad has a place in Holmby Hills and a ranch in Santa Barbara. He said he was heading toward Brentwood. "Want to stop by?" I asked. "There's something I need to talk to you about."

"Is your dad home?" Lucas asked cautiously.

Just then Daddy bellowed for me. "Well, I guess so," I said. "We're just sitting down to dinner. But I'll like gulp and catch you in fifteen, okay?"

I clicked off and ran into the dining room. "Lucas is stopping by." I sat down and poured a scooch of olive oil onto my salad and two drops of balsamic vinegar. "And remember, Daddy. I am not going to the dance with him, so you don't have to see his driver's license or have one of your law clerks research his credit rating."

Daddy stopped eating. "Anything else?" he asked, knife and fork poised in his hands.

I speared an arugula leaf and beamed at him. "Yes," I said. "That cardigan you're wearing is furiously fresh. It makes you look way cuddly, like a total Tickle Me Elmo."

We were starting dessert when the bell rang. I jumped up. "I'll get it, Daddy," I insisted. "It's only Lucas. Lucy!" I hollered, heading for the dining room door. "Is there any ice cream left for Daddy?" I wanted to ensure his remaining at the table for as long as possible.

"I finished the peach. We got some fudge ripple," she called back. "It's all icy though. And kind of yellow around the edges. Which is why I didn't eat it yesterday."

"Thank you, Lucy. Just bring him a dish of something creamy rich and delicious. We must have something," I said. "Oh, and don't worry about getting the door. I'm going—"

"I'm not worried," she yelled. "I'm defrosting an eclair. I'll put in one for your father."

My phone went off just as Lucas and I were settling down in the den. My Baldwin looked so def. He was in Banana Republic corduroys and a collarless pale blue shirt that brutally accented his azure eyes. His floppy blond hair, which he pitched back with a toss of his head, was as strokable as a freshly shampooed golden retriever's. "Excuse me," I said, snapping open my cellular.

It was De. "Well?" she said, anxiously.

"Can I get back to you?" I asked. "Lucas just arrived."

"You're not going to actually do this, are you?" my best bud said, sounding way stressed.

"And by 'this' you mean?"

"Take your pick." She was practically panting. "Hang up on me without reporting what transpired between Murray and the Woo, or talk Lucas into taking Sharon to the Bash," she said. "Either one is heinous."

"In your humble opinion," I noted. "I'll call you back as soon as I can, De. Daddy can do an eclair in two bites. And unless Josh is lulling him to sleep with prelaw trivia, he'll be in here before Lucas and I have our chat, so I've got to go. Did you know you're wheezing?" I asked.

"Actually, I'm viciously hyperventilating. I've like blown out three paper bags since the food court fiasco."

"Try breathing into that little laminated goody bag we got at the Heart Disease fundraiser," I suggested. "It's way resilient—"

"What was he doing with Kimberly?" Dionne shouted.

"De, I've got to go. Details at eleven. I promise," I whispered, and hung up.

Lucas had gotten up and was checking out our CD collection. "The classical stuff and Simon and Garfunkel is my dad's," I said. His hands flew off the disks as if they'd been burned.

"So, um, what I called you about," he began, "is this Raphael guy—"

"I just want to say, before you say anything," I interrupted, "that I hardly even know the boy and had no idea he had this hand-kissing compulsion."

"Yeah, that was seriously weird," Lucas said. "I mean, why would anyone want to do that?"

"Well, I do use a decent aloe lotion with gentle

abrasives to revitalize skin and turn hands invitingly silky," I pointed out. "So it's not like totally surprising that Raph would be drawn to my hands."

"He wants to join the hockey team," Lucas said. "And I'm captain, so I thought I should like check him out."

"Raphael is joining the hockey team?" I don't know why it surprised me so. I just never pictured the pale urban cowboy on skates. "Now, that is seriously weird."

"You think being on the hockey team is weird?" Lucas challenged.

"Not even!" I quickly asserted. "Just Raphael's sudden interest. Lucas, let's not talk about him, okay?" I patted the sofa beside me. "I have this humongous favor to ask of you. You know Sharon Clay—"

His defensively hooded eyes relaxed. "Is she looking slick or what?" he said. Flinging himself onto the sofa beside me, he leaned back, hands cradling the back of his head, excellently toned legs stretched out before him. "I never noticed it until today, but the girl's turning into a basic babe."

I was gratified, of course, but momentarily taken aback.

"I had this little talk with her last week," Lucas continued. "I think that had something to do with it."

"I'm sure you furiously inspired her," I said. "Sharon and I have become close recently."

"Tell me about it." Lucas snorted.

"And as you noted," I continued, "she's like in the midst of this major transition. I see her as a Betty-in-progress, only her ego is frantically fragile and her social skills are Jurassically grunge. What she needs, Lucas, is a vicious esteem builder. Something like—" I paused, peering up at our rough-hewn designer beams as though deep in thought. "Well, like showing up at a high-profile school function on the sturdy arm of a known Baldwin."

He sat up and cocked his head at me. "You mean, like going to some major Alcott bender like the Monster Bash with someone like me?"

"Oh, wow! That is so brilliant. That would totally send her stock soaring," I said, then took a deep breath and went for it. "Lucas, how would you feel about taking Sharon to the Monster Bash?"

"If I didn't have a date with you?" He shut his eyes, lifted his square jaw, and gave the prospect a moment's consideration. "She's not my type," he concluded.

"You said she was a babe," I reminded him. "And, Lucas, this is so important to me."

He stood abruptly and stared down at me in disbelief. "Are you saying," he demanded, raising his voice, "that you want me to like blow you off and take someone else to the Bash?"

"Not just someone else," I said, standing, too. "We're talking about your good friend, Sharon," I said irritably. "And, since *I'm* requesting it, Lucas, it wouldn't be like you were blowing *me* off!"

"No," Lucas said heatedly. "It would be like you blowing *me* off!"

Daddy was at the door in a flash. "Okay, okay, what's going on here? Who is this? Why is my Simon and Garfunkel CD out of the rack?"

"Please, Lucas," I said. But he'd gone pale. He was staring at Daddy, his azure eyes big as Ping-Pong balls. "Please say you'll do it."

"Do what?" Daddy wanted to know.

"I'll do it," Lucas yelled. "Whatever you want. Uhm, sorry about the noise, er, Don Horowitz."

"Not Don, Mel," I whispered.

"It's a term of respect," Lucas said. "And I totally respect you, er, Mel. Cher, I'd be happy to take Sharon to the dance, if that's what you want. Your daughter's happiness is like majorly important to me, sir."

"Daddy, Lucas and I have to talk strategy here. Will you please excuse us?"

"No more raised voices," Daddy warned. "Josh was telling me about this momentous First Amendment case, and I was just dozing off when you kids started hollering."

I glanced at Lucas. His blue eyes were still bulging and completely focused on Daddy. "We'll be so quiet," I promised. "You won't even know we're here."

Chapter 9

You said you'd call. You didn't call. I knew you wouldn't call. I waited and waited!"

Morning light pierced my curtains. With sleep-bleary eyes I blinked at it. I didn't remember hitting the speakerphone button, but there was De's voice heaping shame on me before I'd even showered.

"Can I get back to you?" I kind of whimpered, pulling my Laura Ashley comforter, with its field of delicate pink and white flowers joined by mossy green ivy, over my head.

"Get back to me?" De shrilled. "Oh, you mean, like you did last night? Duh, let me think. Whoops, time's up. The answer is: No, I don't really think so!"

Reluctantly, I slid my feet out from under the duvet and searched with pedicured toes for my fluffy bunny slippers. "Dionne, one: I am seriously regretful over last night's lapse," I said, turning my head phoneward. "But it's not like I was sitting around doing my nails or something. Well, actually, technically, after Lucas left, I was. But it was only because this one french tip was dangerously loose and in need of immediate attention."

"Spare me the manicure melodrama," De barked. "What happened at the mall?"

"Hello, I was getting to that," I explained, shuffling over to my computer to check out the day's wardrobe options. "That was going to be two. Only you are so impatient—"

"Cher!"

"Nothing of consequence!" I snapped back, switching on my PC. "They were looking at this brutally boring book on African-American folktales. And even though Murray slammed it shut when I approached, there was nothing the least bit romantic about the volume or their conference."

Eyes sleepily squinting at the monitor, I pointed and clicked through my ensembles, pausing briefly at a Donna Karan outfit with a revealing jacket geared for the abdominally fabulous. "Time out. What's the shade du jour?" I asked De.

"I'm still into blue tones," she acknowledged with a trace of annoyance, "but moving away from pastel to the cobalt end of the spectrum. Are you like totally sure there was no attraction between them?"

"Murray called the meeting a consultation," I revealed. "How romantic does that sound? Dionne, I did not get love vibe one from the participants."

"And what would my man be consulting Kimberly Woo about?"

"I don't know," I admitted. "But Kimberly did mention that she is still contemplating getting her locks sheared. You know, so she can go to the Bash as Jamie

Lee Curtis, terrorized babysitter. And Murray was strongly supporting the move."

"I don't like this," De mused.

"Dionne, maybe that book Murray slammed shut holds a clue. Perhaps a library visit is in order. I'll even go with you," I offered, clicking through the bountiful selections in my computer in search of an outfit that would complement but not clash with De's palette. "Of course, my morning is way overbooked, but we can do it at lunchtime, right after Lucas keeps his promise." I let the information trail provocatively.

"You did it!" Despite her disapproval, De was impressed. "Forgive my self-absorption, girlfriend. Did you actually talk the Burlinger boy into going to the dance with Sharon? Or should I say Shar?"

"He's slated to ask her at lunch," I responded with pride. "At twelve-thirty. She'll be with me, of course."

"Like Krazy Glue," said De.

"And I'll excuse myself and Lucas will ask her—" Just then my call waiting went off. "Hang on, Dionne," I said, and hurried over to the phone console to click in caller number two.

It was Sharon. "What are you wearing?" she wanted to know.

"De's doing blue. I'm thinking peach or salmon," I replied.

"Let me rephrase that," she said, "What am *I* wearing?"

"I'd go for a pale purple hue," I recommended. "No metal jewelry, no skin piercing. Earth-tone makeup, bu keep it light and frothy. And don't forget to use creme rinse. Catch you later, girlfriend."

I clicked off and returned to De. "It was Sharon, said. "She is going to totally flip when my noble hunk corners her in the cafeteria and asks her to the Monster Bash. Okay, so we'll suit up and assemble on campus."

"Let's synchronize our timepieces," De suggested. "I'm wearing Swatch, blue tennis band."

"I'll do Swatch, too. Smiley face. Fuchsia band."

"We're synched," De said.

At precisely twelve twenty-five, Swatch watch time, De and I stood up and excused ourselves from our patio table in the Quad.

"Where are you going?" Sharon asked predictably. Purple was so the right decision. The little lilac crop top she was wearing with a flaring violet and yellow plaid miniskirt brought out that special feline glow in her eyes.

"Oh, just to get some dessert," De announced with a teasing lilt in her voice. "Can we bring you anything?"

I wanted to pinch her. What if Sharon said yes. Lucas was meeting us inside in less than five minutes. As I'd anticipated, however, Sharon rose. "No, I'll go with you and sort of browse, okay?"

"Totally," I said, taking her arm.

The three of us were standing in front of the ornate brass cappuccino machine in the cafeteria, waiting for Miles to take our latte orders. For dessert, De had selected a plump, million-calorie, nut-infested brownie. It was a desperate act, but given the level of stress she'd been under, I understood and even sympathized with her choice. I opted for fresh strawberries. Predictably, Sharon went the fruit route with me.

Miles and Lucas arrived at exactly the same time.

"Skim milk cappuccino," De ordered, handing Miles her personalized cup.

"Tell him you don't want cinnamon," I reminded her.

Then realizing that Lucas had begun chatting with Sharon, I turned from my forgetful homey and strained to hear their repartee.

Surprisingly, Sharon didn't seem all that interested in what my hockey hunk had to say. She kept glancing nervously at me, silently pleading for direction. I nodded encouragingly. Then, suddenly, I noticed Sharon's eyes spark.

"Princess!" Raphael called to me. "How choice is this, running into you? Wait till you hear what I did for you."

De, a steaming cup of cappuccino in hand, was just turning away from the counter. In his puppy-dog exuberance, Raph jostled her arm. "Watch it," De yelped.

Raph jumped back, pulling me out of the way as the cappuccino, cinnamon-flecked foam and all, splashed out of De's cup onto her blue chenille leggings.

I grabbed a handful of napkins and helped my irate bud blot the espresso stains. As we discarded the wet ones, Raph fed us clean napkins and babbled nonstop about how he'd tried out for the hockey team because he'd noticed I had a thing for athletes. And how nimble was that of him to put himself on the line, risking his limbs to show where his heart was. And now that he'd done this major demonstration of caring, didn't I like owe him?

All the while Raphael was nattering at me, I kept mopping up De's stained leggings and glancing anxiously at Lucas and Sharon. The girl seemed more concerned with what was going on with me than with Lucas's invitation to the dance. She was barely listening to him, the way that I was barely listening to Raphael.

Confused, even distressed, she gazed at me.

"So, like, will you?" I thought I heard Lucas ask her. I nodded my head encouragingly.

"Excellent!" Raphael's fist shot up triumphantly. "The princess said yes! Cher is going to the Bash with me," he announced. "She said yes!"

"I did not," I protested.

But Raphael wasn't listening. He tossed the handful of napkins he was still holding into the air, shouted, "Got to get to hockey practice, princess," and scampered off. But not before he grabbed the sleeve of Lucas's varsity jacket and tugged him away from Sharon. "Come on, captain," Raphael urged. "The rink awaits."

Before Raph pulled him away, Lucas glanced at me. I could hardly meet his gaze. The grimace of anger and hurt that had flared in them when Raphael announced that I was going to the dance with him was crushing. I turned to Sharon, expecting to see a glow, a grin of joy, the beginnings of pride and satisfaction blossoming in her smile. Instead, I met the same betrayed look I'd seen in Lucas's eyes.

But that so did not make sense. "Well, how does it feel," I asked my protégée, forcing enthusiasm into my voice for her sake, "to be going to the bender of the year with Alcott's number one Baldwin?"

Her cat's eyes viciously squinted at me. "How could you do this to me?" she hissed suddenly. "Okay, maybe we weren't like really friends and all. But you were supposed to help me."

Stunned, I tried to protest.

"You'll be sorry," Sharon bitterly cut me off. "Oh, I'll still dress like you," she raged. "I'll use a triple creme hydrating mask at night and milk protein conditioners that uplift even the most flaccid hair. I'll still sign autographs and be like a totally dazzling Betty. But I regret the day I let you trim my split ends and do my color chart. And you will, too," she promised.

Then she flung down her dessert, which splashed all over everything, sending chunks of tropical fruit in all directions, and ran out of the cafeteria.

Dionne shrieked. I turned to her. There was a slice of kiwi on her cheek and a gob of papaya in her hair. I moved toward her.

"Wait!" She held up a hand, stopping me. "I just want to know one thing," she challenged. "Are you going to the library with me?"

"Now?" I asked. "De, I'm too torn up—"

"I knew you were going to do this!" she cried. "You said we'd go after lunch. And now it's after lunch. And you're not going to go, are you?" she demanded.

"Dionne." I reached out to her.

"No!" she shouted, tearing the papaya chunk out of her hair and throwing it to the floor. "You say you'll call me back, but you don't. You tell me you'll go to the library with me. But do you, Cher? No! I tried to warn you about Sharon—"

"Well, I tried to warn you about the cinnamon," I protested.

My best friend's hazel eyes narrowed into this evil squinchie, and turning on her choice suede sandals by Nathalie M., she stalked away.

Chapter 10

*R*ight, like I was supposed to go to class after that? And what, act like everyone I cared about wasn't bitterly bent out of shape and carrying a ten-pound grudge. Hello, not even! Mentally, I ran down the remainder of my day: phys ed, an easy blow off. Art, my attendance was optional. And Ms. Geist's slide show of flood damage in Laguna, a total elective.

In a brutal daze, I drifted across the Quad, barely acknowledging the waves, whispers, and worshipful acclaim of my peers—the ones who were still talking to me. And then my pearlized Charles David pumps seemed to take on a life of their own. Like Dorothy's red shoes, they carried me far from home. Westward along Wilshire I wandered, past chic boutiques and trendy boîtes, onto the turbulent terrain of UCLA. It was midafternoon when I arrived in Westwood, which is a total Oz but with all the munchkins carrying backpacks and wearing Gap.

Unable to continue, my feet aching almost as much as my heart, I slipped into the nearest fern-decked, brick-walled coffeehouse. There, slumping against a leather banquette that probably looked much better in the dim light of evening poetry readings, I ordered an iced latte and paused to take stock.

With a sigh, I thought of Dionne. Although seriously distressed by my best friend's over-the-top reaction, I couldn't dismiss her final rant. She *had* tried to warn me about Sharon. And early on she'd noted similarities between me and the headstrong Victor Frankenstein—like both of us naively believing we'd somehow control our renovated creatures.

Now, I thought as a waitress in a tie-dyed fashion time-warp delivered my latte, Dionne's dire prophecy had come true: Monster turns on maker. Maker is toast.

Plus, between irate best friends, hurt honeys, and postal protégées, maker's social life seemed furiously over. Everyone I cared about was angry at me. Except Daddy. At least, until he found out that the pricey pumps I'd charged to his account had carried me off campus in the middle of the school day. Then he'd probably hop aboard the Trash Cher train, too. Which was so unfair. But—

"Miracles do happen."

For a moment I thought I had dreamed the words. I looked up slowly. Sunshine poured through the coffee-house windows. Shading my eyes, I tried to bring into focus the features of the lanky figure silhouetted against the bright daylight.

"It's Cher, package free. How did you make it through the greater Beverly Hills shopping district empty-handed?" the apparition asked.

Rarely mistaken for an angel, it was Josh, predictably decked out in his cutting-edge, college boy uniform, a flannel shirt and weathered jeans.

"Shouldn't you be in class or like out protesting something?" I said. "There must be an endangered species somewhere around here that needs saving. Go away, Josh."

He sat down. "Speaking of class, how come you're out so early? Is it a holiday?"

"Yes. We're celebrating Backward Day," I replied. "That's when everything you try to do right comes out heinously wrong and the support group you furiously depend on abruptly abandons you."

The tie-dyed waitress swung by just then and put a cup of tea and a tiny teapot in front of Josh. "That's right, isn't it?" she asked him. "You're chamomile with honey."

Josh gave her a grateful grin which came close to justifying the fortune Daddy had spent on his braces. When she left, he stirred his tea. Clearly, my ex-bro was known in the nabe. It felt weird noting that Josh actually had a life. "Rough day, huh?" he said, not looking up at me, which I appreciated.

"Duh, like you thought I was really serious?" I said.

"Did I seriously think it was Backward Day? No," Josh confessed, spooning honey from the bottom of his cup. "Do I seriously want to know why you're not in school, not shopping, not working out, and not bettering the lives of those around you? I'll admit, I'm curious." He let the honey dribble back into his tea, then set down his spoon and took a sip.

"Well, I'm totally fine," I asserted. "Hooked up, loqued out, brutally stoked, and popular as ever. I have not care one in the world. Just this teensy dilemma to work out. Which is why I thought I'd stroll through the IQ-and-Frisbee capital of the poly fleece generation and like try to suck up some problem-solving vibes."

"Whatever you're dealing with, Cher, it must be serious if you'd leave school and trek all the way to Westwood for inspiration." Josh chortled. "So how's your project going?" he added conversationally.

"Amok," I replied, stabbing at my iced drink with a straw. "Like frenzied, out of control."

Josh cleared his throat. "I don't usually do this sort of thing, but if you want me to help you, like with a first draft or something, I'm pretty good with book reports."

"The book report is so not the problem," I confessed. "Thanks anyway."

"Want a lift home?" Josh asked. "I'm heading that way."

I shook my head. "It's too early for me to put in an appearance," I said.

Josh studied me. A look of concern crossed his Baldwinian brow. "So we'll ride around for a while. Come on," he said, picking up the check the Grateful Dead groupie had tossed my way. "We'll go up into the hills. I'll show you how to drive a shift."

"You think I'm like brutally despondent, don't you?" I asked.

"No," my benevolent bro insisted, "I'm looking for a way to increase my metabolism without aerobics."

Josh was driving this yellow Kharmann-Ghia with a rust-coated blue front fender. It was supposed to be this vintage sports car, but basically it was a dilapidated VW. "It's a loaner," Josh explained. "My Laredo's in the shop."

"It's a loser," I corrected. No one I knew was in the vicinity. Still, I slipped on my Web shades and pulled up the collar of my peach silk Joop! jacket as Josh tugged open the passenger side door for me.

We cruised over to Malibu and up into the Santa Monica Mountains, where the rustic compounds of a legion of top-drawer celebs nestle behind electronically guarded gates. With Josh firmly at the wheel, we were searching for Barbra Streisand's rambling complex, when I finally broke down and delivered this dramatic What-I-Did-in-School-Today monologue.

With a sympathetic grunt here and a compassionate nod there, my dad's ex-wife's son took in my every word.

"So Lucas thinks I dumped him for Raphael, who is under the delusion that I agreed to go to the Monster Bash with *him,* which is a blatant As if! Whoops, Josh, there it is!" I pointed out the fabled Streisand mansion with its guest houses and sports facilities, then continued my summary. "And for reasons beyond comprehension, this scenario infuriated Sharon, who turned on me and swore vengeance, which naturally psyched me out, and when I turned to my best friend for solace, Dionne went into this huge oh-you're-getting-on-my-last-nerve thing and hasn't so much as beeped me since."

"Was that really Streisand's ranch?" Josh asked as we careened along the trendy, unpaved road.

"Remind me to share my gut-wrenching difficulties with you again soon." I crossed my arms and sank down in the seat. "You don't get it, do you?" I admonished him.

"Get what? That once again you meddled in other people's lives and that even though you read a classic on the subject, the results were unexpected?"

"That is so cold," I countered as Josh pulled a U-ey on the rugged highway. Sideswiping a roadside cactus, we started back down through the hills. "I just want things to be the way they were before," I confessed. "I want Sharon to be Sharon, not *Shar*. Josh, my situation is way worse than Victor Frankenstein's."

"In what way?" he asked.

"Duh, well, for one, I'm real. I thought you were going to help me."

"Do you want my help?" he asked.

"Hello," I practically shouted. "Why else would I even be seen in this previously owned vehicle with a driver who dresses like a square-dance buff?"

Josh stopped the car so abruptly that a cloud of expensive real estate nearly engulfed it. "Let's try this one more time," he said. "Are you asking for my input?"

"Yes!" I said crisply.

He gave me this big grin. "Great. I'll be glad to help," he said. "I was just waiting for you to ask, that's all. I don't believe in pressing opinions, ideas, color charts, clothing hints, or cosmetic advice on anyone unless they request my help."

"Candidly, Josh," I said, "I am so not asking for your clothing hints, okay?"

He laughed. And there on the hilltop, overlooking the rolling Pacific surf and the palatial beachfront bungalows of the Colony, Josh and I began reviewing my situation. We got out of the Ghia, and I started pacing and talking while Josh leaned against his patchwork car, squinting thoughtfully into the sunlight.

"It's just like in the book," I was saying. "You know the part where the monster follows Frankenstein everywhere? Well, that's exactly what Sharon is doing, only worse. I mean, she doesn't just follow me, she like copies everything I do."

"That's it." Josh straightened up suddenly. "We can work with that."

"What, that she copies me?"

Josh nodded yes. "It's so simple, it's brilliant. You can lead by following, Cher."

"Josh, don't do this to me," I begged him. "I don't know if you're having like a Zen moment or sunstroke, but I totally hate riddles. Plus, I can't drive a stick shift, so if you like wig on me now, we're stuck here in coyote gulch for the duration."

"Didn't you say that you want Sharon to go back to being who she was?" he quizzed me. "Well, if she's going to do everything you do, then you know what you have to do."

"Excuse me? No, I don't know," I insisted. "I have no idea what you're talking about. Of course, she'll do whatever I do, but—" And suddenly I got it. "Not even!" I balked.

"Yep," said the sibling from another planet. "You have to lead the way. Lead her right back to her old life. Lead by example."

"You mean, dress like Sharon used to dress? Go without conditioner? Stick a safety pin through my flawless flesh? I don't think so."

"Okay, kill the safety pin," Josh compassionately agreed.

* * *

We cruised down into the dense rush hour crawl of Pacific Coast Highway traffic. The bluesy sounds of the Wallflowers, featuring Jakob Dylan, the full-out hottie of the Western world, crackled through the VW's ancient speakers. I was heavy into contemplation as we inched homeward. Josh, on the other hand, was thumping on his bandaged steering wheel in this lame attempt to keep time to the music. It was bitterly annoying.

"Hello! I am trying to think," I ventured. "Could you like take up air guitar for a while?" Except for an arch look, I was bitterly ignored. "Could this route be any slower?" I asked a moment later, shifting sullenly in my seat.

"If you walked, it would be," Josh said.

"Oh, thank you. I'm so bad at math," I replied. "Like I never get those 'If a frantic Betty with a Prada purse full of major credit cards and car service vouchers leaves Malibu at the same time as a reconditioned scrap heap on wheels, which one will arrive at 2232 Karma Vista Drive in Beverly Hills first?' questions."

"Okay, Cher. What's the problem, now?" Daddy's favorite prelaw drone snapped off the radio.

"It's Dionne," I said reluctantly. "If you really want to know, I feel I can't make this major transition without her support. She is my homey, my true-blue best friend. And it makes me feel furiously icky to be estranged from her."

"Call her," Josh suggested.

"Oh, right. She has caller ID, Josh. She'd know it was me and like not even pick up. I should have pushed my own pain aside and just gone to the library with her."

Josh was silent.

"Hello," I called. "This is the place where you say, 'That's not your job, Cher. Dionne's a big girl. She can go to the library without you.'"

"What time does it close?" Josh asked.

"The library at school? Oh, it's open late. We have major funding from corporations and trusts fully owned or operated by members of the Alcott PTA. Josh, I've got this furiously golden notion! Can we stop by there now?" I asked. "It would be like this frantic scoop that would totally impress Dionne if I could find out what's in that book Murray was browsing through."

In no time flat, we were out of the Pacific Coast jam, heading inland to Bronson Alcott High. One excellent notion fueled another. I'd been wondering where I was going to get vintage attire of the pre-Shar cut. I mean, who did I know whose apparel choices were as egregiously off base as Sharon's?

It came to me in a flash. I pulled out my cellular and punched in the digits. Amber picked up on the second ring.

"Y'hellow," she sang. "Amber Salk here."

"Amber, hi. It's Cher," I said. "Girlfriend, what do you have in the distressed silk section of your wardrobe? You know, something lingerie-ish, with slightly soiled slip straps, maybe a bias-cut number with an unfurling hem?"

"Cher who?" my close personal pal replied.

"Cher Horowitz, Amber," I crooned. "You know, the one who went with you to the hospital in third grade after you tried to snag a Simply Red tape from Jesse's collection and he shoved you into the ficus tree in Ms. Hillman's room and you threatened to sue the school unless they covered your cosmetic surgery? That Cher," I said.

Josh chuckled.

"Well, excuse me if I had difficulty believing that *that* Cher would be interested in any of *my* timeless ensembles," Amber was saying, "but, as a matter of fact, I do have a few items you might find entertaining."

I rolled my eyes at Josh as the Marilyn Manson of couture launched into a seam-by-seam description of the treasures in her *I Love Lucy* and *That Girl* retrowear collections. Hello, was getting a word in edgewise remotely possible? Not even. I was glued to this fifteen-minute digression on the high-end vintage shops where Demi, Whoopi, and Winona troll for funky Oscar-night garb, when a click on my line indicated that someone was trying to reach me.

"Amber, can I put you on hold for a sec?" I said.

"—And Uma and the Courtneys, Cox and Love, totally scour Julian's on Third for deco couture," she droned on as Josh spun his creaky steering wheel and we wheezed into the school lot.

The facility was nearly deserted. Even the valet parking people were gone. There was only one acceptable vehicle present, a dark Lincoln limousine in which a uniformed chauffeur sat reading *Forbes* magazine.

"Josh, Dionne must be here! I bet she's in the library. That's Clarence, her mom's driver, in that limo," I said. Then, hitting call waiting, I went, "Bueno?"

"Cher? It's De. You'll never guess where I am!" My best bud sounded fully vivacious.

"Oh, let me try, okay?" I squealed happily. It was so excellent to hear her voice in all its lilting enthusiasm. "Is it like a big white building, with marble pillars, and it's got all these wise sayings chiseled into it, like: 'Outside of a dog, a book is man's best friend. Inside a dog, it's too dark to read'? Could it be the new Bronson Alcott Library building?"

"Amazing!" De gasped.

Through the bug-dusted windshield of the Kharmann-Ghia, I saw the library's doors swing open. Cell phone crooked between shoulder and ear, an impressive pile of books in her arms, De emerged into the hazy daylight. "How did you guess?" she was saying. "I did it, Cher! I went to the library. All by myself!"

"Then you're not angry at me?"

"Well, I was," she confessed. "But then Mira said, actually, I should thank you for the opportunity because if you hadn't been so self-absorbed and like bitterly abandoned me, I doubt that I would even have——"

"Excuse me," I interrupted, trying to keep my tone light and breezy. "Mira? Who is Mira?"

As De started down the wide steps, this furious babe in a turtleneck sweater and leather miniskirt exited the library and called to her. The hottie had short, dark Jada curls framing a face as carefree and open as Whitney's before Bobby Brown. And she was like waving this book.

"Our new librarian, Mira Brittany," De cellularly informed me. I watched as she turned to greet the book waver. "Cher, hang on a minute, okay? Hey, Mira. 'Zup?" I heard De say.

Although I was mortified about doing so, I stepped out of Josh's car. Neither De nor our new librarian had noticed it yet, and I hurried across the parking lot toward them, head held defiantly high.

Miss Brittany was speaking animatedly to Dionne. She had just added her book to De's armful. Then gently picking what looked at a distance like a shriveled piece of kiwi off my t.b.'s doeskin-draped shoulder, the miniskirted bookmeister returned to her post.

"Thanks, Mira," De called after her as I got within person-to-person conversational range.

I clicked off my cell phone. "Hi," I said, heading up the steps to help my homey with her book burden.

Dionne shrieked with pleasure. "Girlfriend! What are you doing here?"

"I was on my way to this very venue," I said, "to try to find out about the book Murray and Kimberly were perusing at the mall." I took three of the six volumes she was holding. "De, I'm seriously sorry I bombed out on you."

"And I'm sorry I wigged," she conceded.

We couldn't hug because of the books, but we knocked cheekbones and plied each other with apologetic air kisses, which may not be all touchy-feely but are excellent for like safeguarding makeup.

En route to the waiting limo, De assured me that everything had worked out chronically. Miss Brittany had not only introduced her to the library's excellent computer system, but to this total wealth of African-American folklore. She had also, with De's delicate yet persistent prodding, filled my bud in on a certain sophomore's recent interest in the same topic.

"So now I've got all the books my man's been checking out," De reported. "And one of them is bound to provide clues to his recent bizarro behavior."

Clarence, De's mom's driver, tossed down his financial 'zine and hopped out of the Lincoln to aid us. Across the lot, Josh was waiting. Apparently, his radio was still working. I could see his hands eurhythmically pounding the steering wheel.

"Let's hit my mansionette and research the night away, okay?" De suggested as Clarence took the pile of books from us.

My impulse was to promise her anything. But the Arpège moment passed. "Girlfriend, I can't," I said gently. "Josh is right over there. He gave me a lift." I indicated the aged car lazing in the lot. "Actually, it's this totally recyclable vehicle," I explained when De glanced Josh's way. "You know how environmental college boys are."

"Hey, Josh!" she shouted.

My stepsib interrupted his solo to toss one of his few fans a major grin. I signaled him that I'd be just a moment more and filled De in on the basics of his whack proposal.

"So I'm supposed to like turn myself into a prior version of Sharon," I summarized. "But no matter how high the stakes, hair tampering is out of the question. I am viciously opposed to going without creme rinse to accomplish this."

To my extreme dismay, De fully backed Josh's plan. And when I told her that Amber would be outfitting me for the occasion, her hazel-hued eyes crinkled with mirth.

"Oh, no!" Suddenly, I remembered. "I put Amber on hold!"

De was way amused. "You go, girl," she called as, yanking the slim Motorola out of my cosmetic-crammed backpack, I tore across the parking lot and dove into the Wheels of Shame.

"You cut me off like a designer label at a discount mall!" Amber raved after I'd snapped open my cellular and clicked it back on. "Okay, if you could care less about Golly Ester on Melrose where Gucci's own Tom Ford recently went on a shopping spree, but to leave me dangling like a loose sequin on a Lacroix bustier is ugly!"

"Girlfriend, you're still there?" I said gratefully. "I'm on my way!"

Chapter 11

It was Thursday before I got up the nerve to put Josh's plan into effect and the dregs of Amber's seedy wardrobe on my back. Sheer desperation drove me to it.

I had spent Wednesday trying everything I could think of to relieve Sharon's fury. Asking her to explain what exactly I'd done to earn her rage got me nowhere, and offering to apologize so did not work. I probably did it wrong anyway. I don't actually apologize all that often, so I'm not like an expert at it.

"You're sorry? Don't make me laugh," Shar had scoffed during lunch in the Quad. "When it comes to sorry, Cher, I know sorry. And you are so not sorry."

Other than one-upping me in the apology arena, Shar stayed true to her word. She was wearing this Emporio Armani rayon sheath with midcalf patent-leather boots. It was practically the same color as my Miuccia Prada minidress, only more moss. My Prada was dusty teal, and my boots, though midcalf, were suede with understated Santa Fe-style fringe.

Still, as advertised, my evil twin spent the day trailing me, mimicking everything I said or did, and glaring sullenly at me the rest of the time. Particularly, when Raphael passed us in the hall and hollered something about how he was looking forward to the dance Friday night.

"Raphael, we've got to talk," I responded.

Whereupon Shar elbowed me out of the way and called across the corridor, "Hey, leather man, say hi to my close personal friend Lucas for me, will you?"

"Will do," said the studmuffin. Then looking over his shoulder at me, he winked and went, "See you, princess. And remember, whatever costume you don for the Bash, you've already won first place with me."

I groaned, then turned to confront Sharon. She aimed those angry feline eyes at me. "Come on," she commanded, "or we'll be late for gym. I can't wait to try on this furiously flattering heather spandex workout ensemble I just snagged at the Sweat Shop."

"But I have a heather spandex workout ensemble," I said, starting down the hall toward the sports center.

She fell into step beside me. "Is it a Donna Karan?" she snapped.

I nodded yes. "DKNY," I said.

"What a brutal coincidence," Sharon sneered. "Mine was on sale. Twenty-five percent off!"

The girl was clearly out to destroy me. I had no option. I knew I had to do the unthinkable: Deconstruct the monster I had created, even if it meant dressing badly.

So, Thursday morning I slid my Kula Shaker disk into the CD player for inspiration and, with the post-Oasis

U.K. sensations hitting all the right vintage-Brit-pop buttons, sifted through the stack of seasoned treasures Amber had lent me.

After an agony of indecision, I settled on a short, frosty pink slip-dress, with the merest tear in one side seam. Which totally wouldn't show under the threadbare apple green cardigan I was going to tie around my waist. Slightly torn black mesh thigh highs slipped into faux leopard skin ankle boots completed the major selections.

Despite my earlier pledge, at the last moment, I elected not to shampoo. It was the hardest decision of the morning but so worth it. Since it led me to this dope notion of doing an Olivia Ackst by like darkening my roots with a black marker. Finally, I examined the four braided extensions Murray had lent me. They were excellent. Glossy black and silken to the touch, they felt like Kimberly's hair looked. When I attached them to my limp, day old locks, the effect was outstanding.

I took a wintry spicy-berry route for makeup, which color wise is so not my season. And, as a final gesture, I smeared dark green shadow from a glitter stick over my eyelids. The overall look was triumphantly trashy. If I needed to dive any deeper downscale, Josh had agreed to drive me to school.

He laughed unashamedly as I descended the sweeping marble staircase. I stopped midway and twirled for him. "How not me is this?" I asked.

"Not you to the max," he agreed supportively.

"Tscha!" I said, then cautiously queried, "Is Daddy gone?"

"Left twenty minutes ago," Josh informed me, "after chatting with Hervé, who stopped by."

"Hervé? My kitchen architect?"

Josh nodded. "He's in there now, with sketches for the renovation."

"But who summoned him?" I asked. Continuing down the stairs, I suddenly knew. "Is Lucy with him?"

"She just squeezed some fresh orange juice and fried up a batch of Swedish pancakes for him and is now hand-mashing the berries for his syrup. They're talking color schemes."

Josh ducked into Daddy's den for a moment and I was about to hit the kitchen, but I halted in front of Mom's portrait, instead.

"Ma, you crazy disco chick," I said. I like to use the language of her day when checking in with Mom. "You'll be so proud of me, because I'm off to do a solid. It's kind of this environmental thing. I've got to clean up a toxic dump I built."

Josh was at the front door. "Ready?" he called.

"Later, Ma," I whispered. "Wish me luck."

I tried to talk Josh into dropping me a block away from school, but he insisted on taking me right to the front walk. Ryder Hubbard, the skateboard zero, almost dropped his copy of *Thrasher* when he saw us.

"Rowdy wheels, dude." Ryder was impressed with Josh's trashmobile. "If I like got some air doing a backslide down that nine-stair handrail," the slacker mused aloud, indicating the school steps, "I could do like a punishing ollie over that machine."

"Another fan," I told Josh. "Thanks for the lift."

"Whoa, bummer, Cher." Ryder stared at me as Josh pulled away. "The Monster Bash isn't until tomorrow night. Bet you feel stooged, huh? Coming to school in your costume and all. But it's a jammin' outfit. Definitely in the competition. I give it a nine point two."

"Thank you, Ryder," I replied. "I'm bitterly choked by your support."

"*De* totally *nada,* dude." The wheeled one boarded away, leaving me to hike up the drooping straps of my frosty pink ensemble, tighten the knot in the pilled sweater wrapped around my waist, and go for it.

I have to admit, I was nervous. I had never put in a public appearance anywhere ever with unwashed hair. Let alone clothed in obsolete, previously owned apparel. But striding across the Quad in search of my crew, my discomfort began to diminish.

"Radical streetwear, Cher," Baez called to me. "Two thumbs up," Tai agreed.

I was buoyed by their reactions, yet conscious of their loyalty.

"Could that be Cher? Oh, no!" a redhead in a Fendi sleeveless put a temporary crimp in my confidence. "My mom just cleaned out my grandma's place in Cleveland, and I told her to like trash the clothes." The girl pulled out her cell phone. "I hope it's not too late to stop her."

"If Cher's gone retro," I heard her companion say, "it must be fiercely happening."

It continued like that the entire way across the Quad. So by the time I reached our usual breakfast nook on the patio, I was stoked and eager to touch base with De. Amber was sitting alone at our reserved table, scarfing down a blueberry muffin. "Hey." I twirled for her. "What do you think?"

"You mean besides that every stitch on your back is mine?" She raised her eyebrows, which were dangerously overplucked. "Actually, I think you look frighteningly like the left side of a Sharon Clay before-and-after photo spread."

"That is so affirming," I enthused, actually considering hugging her. Only realizing that the stiff spray in her hair would brutally claw my cheek deterred me. "Yummy-looking muffin," I commented sociably. "So, where's De?"

Amber reddened guiltily. "Clearly, she was finished with her muffin. She left it here totally unattended."

"Amber, I don't care whose muffin it is," I said.

"Well, she's over there." She hitched her thumb in the direction of a small crowd that had gathered like an everything bagel at the edge of the patio. "She and Murray are doing their famous To Trust or Not to Trust soliloquy. And Sean is getting top dollar scalping orchestra seats. Seems that everyone has brutally missed their performances."

De and Murray arguing again? I stretched and tried to peer over the heads of the crowd, but my mesh stockings had like no give.

"Research? Not even." I recognized my best bud's spirited remarks. "I've got the four-one-one on your follicle foraging missions." The words—De's words— "And I am not your shorty," rose heatedly above the crowd's shouts of encouragement.

I was way distressed. My t.b. had taken an oath not to publicly air her trust grievances. She'd zipped her lip against brutal odds for nearly two weeks. Tomorrow was the Monster Bash and the end of her moratorium with Murray. I couldn't believe she'd blown it with just twenty-four hours to go.

"Who or what are you trying to be?" a condescending voice demanded.

I whirled around. It was Sharon. She was wearing a choice strapless sweater that was nearly identical to the Sonia Rykiel I'd looked at longingly that morning, and the trippin'est little stiletto heels Manolo Blahnik ever cobbled. I felt a twinge of envy—which was icky and so foreign to me—as her cat's eyes took in my outfit in minute detail.

Tossing my head, so that the extensions I'd clipped on fanned out like broken umbrella spokes, I smiled. "It's my new look," I said.

"What, like you're off Revlon and into Crayola now?" She stared at my inky roots, horrified. "Yuck. When was the last time you even rinsed that mop?" Confusion replaced contempt in her glance. "I don't get it. Why would you want to look like that?" Sharon asked, indicating her own healthy, shining hair, her subdued makeup, the outrageously golden Rykiel sweater and matching skirt she was wearing, "when you could look like this?"

Amber was watching us, wide-eyed.

"Sharon, can we talk privately," I suggested.

"Why? Are you going to try to apologize to me again?" she sneered. "Duh, who was it who once advised, 'You don't want to push politeness all the way to groveling, which is so unattractive'?"

"Sounds like Cher," Amber offered.

To her credit, Sharon shot the stiff-haired one a wilting glare. I had taught the girl well.

"Excuse me, but this is so not a public conversation, Amber," I said. "Perhaps you can find some other abandoned pastries to snack on while Shar and I continue our discussion."

I took a chance and stormed away. A moment later I heard Sharon's voice at my back. "Are you really going to class like that today?" she demanded. "Because if you are, I don't think I want to accompany you. You're totally going to destroy our reputation."

Just then Kimberly came by, with all her hair tucked

up into this fuzzy blue ski cap with the earflaps hanging open—which I recognized at once as Sean's. It looked frantically cute on Kim.

"Chronic duds, girlfriend," she called to me. "Are you doing that raw, colorful, highly individualized, eighties thing like in the style of New Wavers like Annabella of Bow Wow Wow?"

"It's hip, young, and even a little trashy, isn't it?" I trilled back. "Love that cap."

As Kimberly took off, Sharon hurriedly caught up with me. "She actually liked your attire?" my former acolyte mused, astonished.

"You were saying?" I challenged.

"Why are you dressed that way?" Her shoulders had begun to slump. "Is it really your new look?"

I put my arm through hers and steered us instinctively toward the playing fields. "I'm just testing it out," I confessed. "It's a frenetic mix of textures, colors, patterned tights, and ethnic jewelry, all tossed together with the offhanded coolness of an easy rider, don't you think?"

"Well, it is kind of free spirited," Sharon reluctantly conceded. "With this chic biker girl edge that would look way fresh firing up a vintage Ducati motorcycle."

"Shar, that's good." I beamed, climbing the steps of the bleachers.

We slid into a fourth-row bench and sat down, side by side. Somewhere before us, the hockey team was doing calisthenics, but I hardly noticed.

"Girlfriend," I began, "I am not going to apologize again. I mean, I'm truly terrible at it anyway. What I really want to talk to you about is the importance of individuality," I continued gently. "Of being yourself instead of someone else—no matter how choice a Betty the other party may be. Because honoring what is special and unique about your own style, taste, looks, and life is so—"

"The forces of destiny are at work again." Sharon and I looked up at the same time. "Hey, princess," said Raphael. He was in his hockey sweats, dark hair wet from his workout. Flushed with athletic exertion, his once-pale face was more than ever a golden setting for those choice green eyes. Which, unless I was mistaken, were fastened on Sharon.

"Oh, hi, Raphael." I acknowledged him without enthusiasm.

He stepped back suddenly. "Are you talking to me?" he asked, looking from Sharon to me and back again. "Cher?"

"Shar," Sharon corrected, smoothing her classic skirt and gazing up at him with a face that looked effortlessly radiant and not the product of my subtly perfect makeup techniques—which is what it so was.

"Oh, wow, really?" Raph was way perplexed. He turned to me again. "So then, you must be . . . ?"

I gave him a wink, dislodging a cascade of sparkles from my upper lid. Flecks of glitter fell like green dandruff onto my shoulder.

"What happened to you?" Raphael wanted to know. "Yo, what's going on here?"

"Cher was just telling me how important it is to be oneself and how shallow things like makeup, clothing, moisturizers, and accessories can be," Sharon reported.

"You didn't believe her, did you?" Raph asked urgently. "I mean, you're not going to let yourself go the way she has, are you?"

"Never," said Shar, accepting Raphael's hand and standing.

"You want to go to the dance with me tomorrow night?" he asked her.

"It's a possibility," Sharon replied coyly. "Beep me later. We'll talk."

"Are you like seriously blowing me off for the Monster Bash?" I asked. I couldn't even pretend to be insulted. My heart totally rejoiced. Suddenly, I saw clearly what I should have known all along. It was Raph whom Sharon coveted.

"I'm sorry," he said now, his green eyes cleanly locked on her tiger orbs. "The kind of guy I am, I gotta go where my heart leads."

"No problem, Raphael," I assured him.

He glanced at me then. "You're a pal," he said, and jogged off to the locker rooms.

"So," I said, standing, "it's Raph you were crushed on, not Lucas, right?"

"Totally," Sharon replied, ferociously grinning.

"Then why did you—"

"Flirt with your hockeymuffin?" she finished my thought. "You taught me to do that yourself. Defensive flirting, remember? You said I should toy with one boy in order to pique the interest of another."

"And that's why," I marveled, putting the pieces together, "when Raph asked me out, you brutally freaked. You weren't interested in Lucas at all."

"Not even." Sharon shook her head.

"I wish I'd known. It would've been so perfect. You would be going to the Bash with Raphael tomorrow night, and I'd be where I belong, in Lucas's lean and proper arms," I said, sighing. "But, of course, now you've got to go with Lucas, right? Because you said yes to him before Raphael asked you."

"As if!" Sharon barked.

"Excuse me?" I blinked at her. "You can't break your date with Lucas. I mean, his ego's already mashed because I broke a date with him, and now if you do the same thing—well, it's too cruel. You can't do it."

"Can't," Sharon quoted me, "is totally not a word in my dictionary of life." Then she turned on her Blahniks and with a bitter "Tscha!" stalked away.

I stared out at the sports field, trying to center myself. I could tell that my chakras were fiercely unaligned. I should have been happy at Sharon's display of sullen independence, I told myself. The Velcro vixen I'd created was no longer my clone. And, I mean, a part of me *was* happy, even proud, that she'd finally taken off on her own. But then, this other part was like seething at her rampant insensitivity and how she kept crediting me with teaching it to her.

I glanced out at the playing field and thought I saw Lucas doing trunk curls with his peers. The sight of him, if it was him, seized my heart like a burning glove of guilt. I wanted to run to him. Not in faux leopard boots, however, with unwashed two-tone hair. But even if I had been appropriately attired, I knew I couldn't do it. I couldn't bear to tell him that the girl I'd fixed him up with was going to the Bash with the boy he thought I'd thrown him over for.

Still tense as the school bell tolled, I began my leaden march back to class. I was like so in another world that I barely heard my cellular go off. And when I finally noticed its muffled ring, I forgot where I'd stashed it. Which is like misplacing your DNA. But finally I dug it out of the belly of the bear and clicked on.

"Girlfriend, where are you?" De's voice was rabidly upbeat. "What a jammin' A.M. I've had. I wish you could have seen us."

"I did," I confessed as a trio of casually attired Calvin kids, like all bone-skinny in these excellently tailored jackets and trousers in subdued charcoal tones, clamored around me. "I caught a few minutes of your patio duet with Murray," I told De. "Can you hold on a sec?"

I turned to the threesome, two girls and a boy, who were marveling at my outfit. "*Vogue* calls it Savage Chic," I improvised. "It's an easy, eclectic, post-generational look."

"Sign my shirt," the boy said, handing me a marker and ripping open his jacket to bare his clean cK T-shirt at me. I scrawled "Cher" with a flourish.

"That's all for now, guys," I told them, returning the pen. "De, are you still there? So, did Murray brutally freak when you broke your word and confronted him in public?"

"No, we're still a lock," she reported happily. "This morning's fracas was strictly a publicity stunt. Murray is determined to win first prize for most original costume tomorrow night. We were just drumming up interest in the event. Anyway, I told you I wouldn't challenge my man or ask him questions to which I did not already know the answers."

Mindlessly, I stroked the braided black extensions Murray had lent me. "You mean you found out why he's been scrounging hair pieces?"

"Those books I borrowed from the library were the key," De reported. "The one on African masks gave me the first hint. All of a sudden, I realized we were into a costume thing, not another woman."

"I knew it," I said, waggling my digits at the pep team as they charged past me, heading for the gym. Chewing on her pencil, notebook in hand, Amber, their poet laureate, was bringing up the rear.

"De was totally finished with that pastry," she called defensively. "Oh, and she's looking for you."

"Thanks. I'm on with her now." I indicated the phone. "Amber," I told Dionne.

"Be grateful," she said. "Without her, my daily calorie intake would fully double. Anyway, that last volume Mira pitched my way was a book of Southern ghost stories," De continued excitedly. "She said that Murray had been psyched about this one tale she'd mentioned to him. And I found it in the book!"

"Not even!" I said, starting up the school steps.

"Even!" De chirped. "It's a classic African-American yarn about a boy named Wiley, who's like afraid of everything. But finally, you know, to confront his fears, he decides to track down this major monster. It's supposed to be the scariest creature ever, a brutally bloodthirsty swamp thing. And there was this ferocious drawing of him. I guess he was supposed to be dripping swamp guck or Spanish moss or whatever. But it looked just like—"

"Hair?" I interrupted.

"Bingo!" said De. "And this famous Southern swamp monster is known as—"

"The Hairy Man!" we hollered together.

"De, wasn't that the monster Murray was telling us about the day Sean swapped his hat for my V.C. Andrews collection?" I asked, swinging through the school doors.

"My man's been collecting hair pieces for his costume, that's all. Once I realized that, the rest fell into place." She was at the far end of the corridor, signing autographs at her locker. It looked like her dramatic improv with Murray this morning had been a smash hit.

"What about Kimberly?" I queried.

"I can't tell you," she said. "I promised. You'll see tomorrow night."

If someone had pulled the plug on the swamp creature's habitat, it could not have drained faster than my enthusiasm. "Not unless they televise the event," I told my pumped pal.

De had extricated herself from her fans and was waiting for me. "Aren't you slated to go with Raphael?" she asked, clicking off cellular.

"He changed his mind because of the way I look," I confessed, snapping shut my mobile.

"Everyone's a critic," De said consolingly.

"And guess who he asked instead? Sharon."

"No!" De gasped. Then she put it in perspective for me. "That is so perfect!" she said.

Chapter 12

"What are you doing home?" Josh stuck his head into the den, where I was reviewing *Frankenstein*.

"Reliving a true classic horror tale," I replied. "'Cinderella.'"

"I don't get it." Stepping uninvited into the room, he scratched his casually coiffed head. "It's Friday. You're never home Friday. And isn't tonight the big dance?"

"Duh, now do you get it?" I asked, flouncing into Daddy's favorite armchair. "No date, no dance."

"No kidding," Josh said, circling behind the chair to check out my reading material. "So what are you doing?"

I closed the book with a bang. "Well, before you strayed in here, I was going to spend the evening polishing my book report for Mr. Hall's class. I mean, since my best friends, not unlike Cinderella's sisters, are at this very moment on their way to the event of the season without me—"

"What happened with Sharon?" Josh sat down on the sofa across from me and filled his fist with popcorn from the bowl on the table between us. "Last I heard, you were going to cut her loose."

"I did." I put down my book and notepad. "Your plan worked so well that my safety date decided to go to the dance with her instead of me. Actually, Josh," I said, leaning forward to cadge a low-cal treat before the bro emptied the bowl, "they were made for each other."

"What about Lucas?" he asked. "I thought he was taking her."

Just the mention of the noble hunk I'd talked into dumping me brought on like hives of regret. I had seen the Baldwin twice since Sharon's defection, once in the corridor during change of class and once crossing the Quad. Both times we'd briefly locked eyes and Lucas had angrily looked away. I shrugged now and threw the popcorn back into the bowl, my appetite suddenly gone.

"Sharon brutally unloaded him," I admitted, throwing myself back into the deep cushions of the oversize chair.

I waited for Josh to comment, but he didn't say anything. He seemed more thoughtful than surprised. Finally, I filled the silence with "So, what are you doing tonight?"

It wasn't until the question was out of my mouth that this shadow of a scheme crossed my mind. I kind of blinked and focused in on him differently.

Survey said: tall, relatively articulate, and considered among coffeehouse waitresses and some of my more generous peers a viable hottie. Of course, he was dressed in his usual lumberjack leisure wear. But then, the dance was a costume ball.

"Why are you looking at me that way?" Josh demanded.

"What way?" I asked.

He stood up abruptly. "I don't know, I just had this creepy feeling that you were going to dive across the table and style me or something."

"As if," I said in this annoyed tone. "I was just trying to figure out what that meandering line in your hair was supposed to represent. Whoops, it's a part, isn't it? How radical would it be to actually use a comb?"

"You never learn, do you?" The boy was staring down at me, shaking his head.

"Excuse me for having this viciously vulnerable moment," I said. "I was just thinking about asking you to go with me to the Bash."

"No," Josh said with a decisiveness that startled me.

"That is so unoriginal," I countered. "I mean like, take a number, please. You have to wait your turn to not take me to the dance tonight!" I turned my head away and buried my face in the upholstery.

"I just don't think it's a solution," Josh began, then added softly, "Cher, are you crying?"

"No!" I shouted, but my voice was muffled by the cushion. "I'm doing a skin peel the hard way. Crushed velvet. It's like the latest tool in dermabrasion."

He laughed. And then I did. I turned around. "Really, you won't go with me?" I asked, rubbing my nose where it had been smushed against the pillow.

"I don't know." He sat back down and picked up the book.

"Yuck. Put that thing down before it strikes again," I urged. "That lame story started all this."

But Josh was flipping through the pages. "Maybe the answer's here, too," he said. "I mean, if Mary Shelley was the cause of your misery, she owes you some relief."

"Mary Shelley didn't recommend the book," I reminded him.

He gave this annoying little chuckle and kept perusing the pages. Then he stopped and looked sideways at me. "What's the one thing Victor Frankenstein never did?" he asked.

"Shop Rodeo Drive, surf Deadman's Curve." I ticked off the events on my fingers. "Do brunch at the Beverly Wilshire. Duh, I give up."

"He moaned and groaned and felt sorry for himself," Josh said, "but he never took personal responsibility for—"

"Spare me," I cut him off. "I mean, you wouldn't be on the verge of offering me unsolicited advice, would you?"

"Okay. I was just trying to help," he said, closing the book. He looked about ready to bail.

Normally, Josh's evacuation would've been no big deal. Tonight, however, I was sensing a trend. I couldn't believe I'd succeeded in getting one more person to abandon me. "No, wait," I said. "Okay, if you need an invitation, you've got it. Please ruin my life again."

Josh grinned. Fortifying himself with more popcorn, the stepsib sat back and slowly spun his theory, which basically was that Frankenstein's sin was arrogance. He created a monster who went out and wreaked major harm and havoc upon others.

"Including and especially Victor's main love interest," I reminded him. "The similarities are fully glaring. First the monster acted like he thought Elizabeth, Vic's beloved boo, was majorly choice, right? Then he crushed her. Not unlike Sharon's callous misuse of Lucas," I noted.

"Okay," Josh said, "but let's focus on Victor. His creature is tearing up the place. So then, seeing the error of his ways, what did the obsessed scientist do? Instead of taking personal responsibility for meddling with the natural process, he blamed the monster. But he never repaired the damage. He never apologized—"

"Bhhaap!" I made the you-got-it-wrong quiz show noise. "There it is, the A word again. Been there. Done that. No way, Josh," I asserted. "I am totally the world's worst apologizer. I tried it with Sharon and was bitterly rebuffed. Plus, what would I apologize for?" I queried irritably. "She got what she wanted. Raphael is taking her to the dance."

"What about Lucas?" Josh asked. "First you said you'd go to the Bash with him, then you talked him into asking Sharon, then she dumped him, too. That's pretty rough on a guy's ego. And you're sitting around blaming Sharon. But who messed with the natural process?"

I flung out my arms and fell back against the cushions. "I'd rather have dental laminates installed than admit this, Josh, but you may be right. Hockey hunks have feelings, too—especially Lucas, who is like your majorly sensitive hottie and did me this brutal solid by asking my protégée to the Bash." I sat forward again and dropped my head into my hands. "But now he won't even speak to me," I said, peering at Josh through my fingers.

"He doesn't have to speak to you, Cher," he said, standing up to leave. "You have to speak to him."

"To apologize?" I asked, sensing the onset of a major wuss attack.

"Yup," said the UCLA cowboy, grabbing a last handful of popcorn. Then he left me, with nothing but eight unpopped kernels rattling in the bottom of the bowl.

I pulled myself up and went to the phone. I knew if I waited, I'd never make the call. Be brave, be brave, I kept going as I dialed Lucas's house. And then I went like, don't answer, don't answer. And he didn't. His machine picked up. The sound of my calendar boy's mellow voice asking me to leave a message put me into brutal meltdown. I couldn't do it. I hung up before the beep.

It was a toss-up: turn over my belt, shoelaces, and any sharp objects to Josh and hide in my room, or phone De. The latter was way easier, especially since I only had to press two buttons to speed dial my homey.

"Cher?" Dionne's caller ID took me by surprise again.

"Hey," I said glumly. "So where are you?"

"We're at the dance. Murray and Sean are circulating and Amber's whitening her face—"

"Excuse me?"

"She came as Elvira," De explained.

"I thought Kimberly was going to be Elvira," I said.

De laughed conspiratorially. "No, she's coming as Jamie Lee Curtis, the babysitter from *Halloween*."

"But Jamie Lee's 'do was merely shoulder length in that flick," I pointed out.

"Kimberly chopped her locks," De eulightened me. "She's been wanting to cut her hair for ages but didn't have the nerve. Sean and Murray supported the move and talked her into donating her leftover locks to them. Sean had to promise her his favorite lid."

"The blue fuzzy," I remembered. "She was wearing it yesterday."

"Girlfriend, I wish you were here," De said.

"Is Lucas?" I cautiously inquired.

148

There was a pause as De perused the room. "At the refreshment table," she said, "which is lavishly loaded with way decent treats. It looks like the leftovers from Jesse's bar mitzvah."

"Is Lucas with anyone?" I asked.

"He's surrounded by Bettys," De confided. "But the boy seems terminally blue."

"Not even." It was a bittersweet revelation. "Like how blue?"

"Why don't you come down and check it out yourself? Everyone is here. The costumes are killin'. The sounds are fierce. It's a proper blowout, girlfriend, yet somehow empty without you."

"Really?" I whimpered.

"Like, duh," she replied.

"De, you're the best. Snag me some hors d'oeuvres before Amber hits the buffet," I said. "I'm on my way."

The speed and skill with which I assembled myself put me in the running for the Guinness book. I hit the button on my rotating clothes rack, shut my eyes, pressed stop, and opened them. What greeted me was a dynamite velvet mini with long tight sleeves that ended in these totally poetic, floppy cuffs. I knew at once which wicked wide-brimmed hat decked with roses would fully kick it. And of course I had already purchased excellent strappy sandals to match.

Josh's look as I came down the stairs was furiously affirming. Even before he executed his official thumbs up, his pupil dilation factor was, Wow! In keeping with my fairy tale fantasy, he drove me to the ball. So it wasn't exactly a pumpkin I stepped out of, more like a squash, but I was feeling way Cinderella as I entered.

The gala, as De had reported, was brutally charged.

Between the cutting edge music provided by Jesse's dad's hottest new group, and the excited screams the costumes were eliciting, the decibel level was frantic. The outfits themselves were awesome.

Like Murray, De had opted for a literature-based ensemble. She'd decided to go as The Raven by Edgar Allan Poe. I thought I caught a glimpse of her sleek and gleaming black feathers near the buffet and headed in that direction.

Moving through the manic crowd was amazing. Masked dancers slapped me high fives and called out greetings as I wove through the fray. Adorably decked out in Munster garb, Mr. Hall and Ms. Geist were doing an energetic shuffle. I ran into Olivia, who was in the astronaut costume Sigourney Weaver wore in *Alien*. She'd sacrificed her nose ring for authenticity. Baez and Tai were wearing nearly identical turn-of-the-decade ensembles.

"Who are you?" I called to them.

"I'm Bridget Fonda; she's Jennifer Jason Leigh," Tai yelled.

"As if," Baez shouted. "She's Jennifer. I'm Bridget."

I recognized the stars of the chiller in which a demented girl starts taking over her roommate's life. *"Single White Female!"* I hollered.

Then I spotted Kimberly in a striped body shirt and bell-bottom jeans doing her *Halloween* thing. Her hair, which she'd tinted a fresh Jamie Lee auburn, had been excellently shorn. It moved with vicious body and bounce as she danced with Sean, who was in this webby garb.

"Spiderman?" I guessed as I passed the rockin' couple.

Kimberly shrugged. "It's ethnic, I think."

"I am Ananta, the spider." Sean danced over and made humorously threatening gestures. "I am the trickster. The shape changer—"

"The what?" I hollered, cupping my ear.

"Yo, I can change shapes," he shouted at me.

"That is a money-in-the-bank skill," I assured him. "Where's Murray?"

Sean pointed somewhere behind me. I turned. And screamed. Murray, if indeed it was my best friend's honey, was like a walking wig store. And woven into the copious hair pieces cascading from his head, shoulders, and arms were twigs, leaves, gelatinous slime, and what I hoped were faux insects. Legions of iridescent roaches, beetles, and water bugs studded his hairy limbs like sequins.

"Eeeewww!" I screeched again.

"Am I the best?" Murray laughed. The sight of his smile-crinkled mustache was furiously comforting.

"That is the most excellent costume ever!" I concurred.

"Better even than my main vampire man?" Murray shouted, clapping the shoulder of the elegantly caped stranger standing beside him.

It was Lucas.

None of the hotties in *Interview with the Vampire*— Brad, Christian, Tom, and Antonio—could hold a candelabra to my blazing Baldwin. His thick blond hair was slicked back and there was this soft mist of pale powder on his crushingly handsome face, which made those timber wolf eyes unbearably choice. They were fixed on me now.

The dancers around us became a colorful blur. The strident music seemed to dull. I got this woozy rush. "Lucas," I managed to say, "you look classic."

"Thanks," he said stiffly. "So, what are you supposed to be?"

I closed my eyes for a sec and took a breath. And then the words just like tumbled out of me. "A bright, sought-after, yet grievously misguided Betty, whose recent behavior reeks," I said. "In other words, myself."

Lucas just watched me. "What's that supposed to mean?" he asked.

"It means I'm sorry, Lucas." I felt like crying. Which, although it had a certain manipulative appeal, was so not an option in this pulsing public arena. The effort not to blubber pushed me into the defensive zone. "Do I have to spell it out?" I added miserably

"Well, yeah," he said, a grin slowly cracking the powder on his choice Baldwin face.

"Duh, I'm apologizing," I explained. "I mean, you asking me to the dance, and me saying yes was a totally natural occurrence which I should never have meddled with. Whereas, my asking you to dump me and take Sharon, although it came from a generous impulse, was a brutally irresponsible act."

"So, you want to dance?" he asked.

"Extremely," I said.

The music rose majestically as we moved into each other's arms. And then the beat got frantic. We moshed with a vengeance, bumping into friends, laughing, shouting conversationally at one another. Rivulets of sweat cut through the white makeup on my vampire's chronic face. His scarlet-lined cape flared dramatically, wrapping around me now and then like a satin cocoon.

De whirled past us in Murray's shaggy embrace, her costume as glamorous as his was grisly. We bumped into Amber, literally. She was downing the remains of a hot dog and chatting with Ryder, who had his arm draped over Tai's shoulder. Amber's black Elvira wig was streaked with mustard, and Ryder was eyeing it hungrily. "I'm making a powder room run," Tai said. "Any interest?"

I excused myself, and we started through the crush. It took us forever to navigate the extravaganza. Mr. Hall had climbed onto the stage and signaled for the band to wind down before Tai and I were halfway across the floor. We stopped where we were and turned to listen to him as the crowd surged forward expectantly.

"I think we can all agree that this has been the best Monster Bash yet," he was saying, looking extremely adorable in his baggy black Munster suit. "And I have the names of our very creative winners right here. But before we announce our costume awards, there are so many people to thank—"

"NOT EVEN!" the audience roared.

But Mr. Hall droned on. I stood on tiptoe and spotted Lucas jock-bonding with two hockey teammates. De wasn't too far from him, just closer to the bandstand, her fabulous feathered arms wrapped supportively around her man. I tried to catch her eye, but she was oblivious.

Finally, when everyone was either comatose or borderline postal and tossing hors d'oeuvres at the stage, Mr. Hall began to announce the prize winners. De craned her neck, searching for me.

When he got to "And now the moment you've all been waiting for!" I grabbed Tai's hand, and we shouldered and squiggled through the rowdy throng, heading for our homey. We were almost there when Mr. Hall tapped the microphone for silence.

"Our grand prize winner for most original costume. The judges' decision is unanimous. Come on up, Murray. The winner is . . . The Hairy Man!"

The ballroom exploded with applause. Kids were whistling and yo-ing and going, "Murr-ay! Murr-ay!" De planted an ecstatic buzz on her man's cheek. Dreads flying, he charged up to the stage. Screaming, Tai and I jumped on Dionne. Then Amber charged through the crowd and flung herself into our victory squeeze. The four of us hugged each other and jumped up and down as Murray, beaming, accepted his trophy and frantically pumped Mr. Hall's hand.

"Show them that costume," Mr. Hall encouraged.

Murray was triumphantly waving the silver trophy. Suddenly, he did this little moonwalk move, then spun around. His swamp creature accessories shook loose, sailing out into the audience. Fat roaches and fuzzy faux spiders went flying as he twirled. Kids were screeching hysterically as the rubber bugs boinged off them. Everyone wigged. This major insect-flinging bender ensued. It took Tai and me ten minutes to wade through the melee and make it to the lounge.

I had splashed some water onto my face and was searching for my hairbrush when Sharon walked in. She was wearing this exquisite turquoise unitard, a little fur-trimmed cap, and carrying a pair of Rossignol skis. She caught me assessing the outfit.

"Christie Brinkley," she said.

"It's supposed to be a horror theme," I reminded her.

"The girl blew off this long-term fairy-tale relationship with a gazillionaire rock star to marry this stooge on a ski slope and then like got divorced two minutes later. I think that qualifies her. So," she said in this perky voice, "I saw you with Lucas. Like, everything really worked out, right?"

"Frantically festive," I conceded. "And you and Raph are a lock?"

"The boy worships me." This huge smile broke out on her face, reminding me of what basically excellent teeth she'd always had. "And of course I couldn't have done it without you."

I was about to politely protest that, really, she had been an exceptional student, but the girl gushed on.

"You were like this sculptor smoothing off my rough edges," she declared. "You know, like an artist chipping away at a perfect block of rare marble to release the glorious work of art locked inside."

I was glad we were near a sink. I have a very strong gag reflex. Tai was standing next to me, repairing her makeup. "I think of Cher as an artist, too," she said, echoing Sharon's grandiose tone. "But more like a starving artist chomping into this ripe apple and finding a worm."

Sharon's grin wavered, but she hurried on. "Anyway, we both got what we wanted, didn't we? I mean, you're here with Mr. July. And my plan to snag Bronson Alcott's premier hottie, Raphael, totally worked."

"Excuse me?" I said. "You mean catching Raph's attention was not merely a makeover bonus but the basic reason you requested my help?"

"Bingo," said Sharon. "I so hope you don't feel used, Cher. It's just that Raphael seemed so drawn to your type"—she busied herself picking invisible lint off the hip of her unitard—"that I had to become as much like you as possible."

Tai shuddered. "That is the total essence of *Single*

White Female," she remarked, then blotted her lips and left us.

"The only reason I dogged your trail," Sharon continued, "was because where you were, Raphael would be."

"Sharon, why didn't you just tell me from the beginning," I asked, "that Raph was your Baldwin of choice?"

"Oh, and like you would have really helped me then," she said sarcastically. "Like you wouldn't have brutally freaked because you weren't totally targeting him for a takeover yourself, right?"

Slip into your P.J.'s, girlfriend, I almost blurted out, because you are so dreaming. But I courteously exercised restraint and just stared at her, amazed.

And this weird thing happened.

I mean, there was this spectacular, spandexed creature standing before me. It was hard to even imagine her as the disheveled grunge queen who'd risked tetanus for a misguided accessory choice. Yet I suddenly flashed back to how the girl had looked less than two weeks ago. The change was uncanny, more like a miracle than a makeover.

From a hopeless, moping bozo addicted to apologizing, Sharon Clay had become a spirited, self-assured, annoyingly obnoxious beauty. Of course, she didn't know how to handle being a gracious Betty yet. That would come with time. But, irritating as I found her new independence, something inside me thrilled to her spunk. I found myself smiling.

"So I just did your bidding, is that what you're saying?" I asked. "And like what—you're taking full responsibility for your admittedly awesome transformation?"

"Credit," she corrected me, beginning to smile herself.

We were at a crossroads. I saw this real choice. I could howl, "As if!" and point out the astounding contributions I'd made to her def conversion. Or I could step back and stop playing Frankenstein.

Like, duh, major decision.

"I can live with that," I said.

We stood there for a second, Betty to Betty. Then Sharon set her little ski cap at a rakish angle and, turning her smile to the mirror, checked her teeth for lipstick. "Raph must be wondering where I am," she confided. "He's way possessive."

"And why not?" I proposed. "He's found his perfect match."

We returned to the fiesta together. Murray was winding down his acceptance speech. He'd borrowed a lot of books and even more hair and had a lot of people to thank.

"Well, kiss, kiss, I'm bailing," Sharon shouted over the bored crowd's hisses and jeers. We knocked cheekbones, and our paths diverged. She moved toward her personal Freddy Krueger. I slipped comfortably into Lucas's warm arms.

Chapter 13

Monday morning everyone was still pumped on how excellent the Monster Bash had been. So poor Mr. Hall was having a hard time getting the class to settle down. "Okay, who wants to be first up with a book report?" he was calling. "Ryder, are you prepared?"

"He's just finishing up." It was Tai's voice, muffled because she had a barrette clamped in her teeth. She was doing Baez's hair.

"Yo, here." Ryder reacted belatedly to hearing his name called.

"I know you're here, Ryder. We established that during attendance. I'm asking if you're ready to present your book report."

"Five minutes, Mr. Hall. I'm like almost there." He held up the magazine he was reading as evidence of his sincerity.

Amber glanced up from gluing her nails and brutally gagged. "Yuck, what is that?" she demanded.

"The new *Fangoria*," Ryder said. "It's got all this insider info on horror films, like this issue has an extremely incisive piece on how they get flesh to look viciously shredded."

"I'll do it," Murray volunteered, standing. He was clutching his trophy.

Everyone started to throw things at him. "Sit down, you did yours at the podium Friday!" Jesse hollered.

Murray looked hurt. "That was my acceptance speech," he reminded them.

"Hello, in addition to your parents, teachers, librarians, and haberdashers, you thanked the Lele and Kuba tribes of Zaire, if I got it right," Baez droned.

"And related this riveting Dogon myth about Ogo, the rebellious trickster," Olivia added.

"And that was all before you thanked the twenty-eight friends and their extended families who donated extensions, falls, ponytails, and wigs to your worthy cause. Next!" Amber called.

"It takes a village to win a trophy," Murray grumbled, brandishing his prize.

"Cher?" Mr. Hall called hopefully.

Standing, I removed my floppy-brimmed hat, which totally matched the cornflower blue of my jacket. Then, shaking out my freshly laundered, streaky blond hair, I gathered my notes and amidst whistles and applause took my place at the podium.

"Okay," I said, smoothing down my alluring Dolce & Gabbana lace knit miniskirt, "this is the story of Frankenstein, who most people think is a monster, but who is really the scientist who created the monster. Against the excellent advice of his close personal friends, Victor

Frankenstein actually succeeded in giving new life to this angry and ultimately ungrateful being."

There was this snicker from Amber's area, and I heard De clearing her throat.

"At first, he was totally psyched because his experiment worked," I quickly continued. "Then, suddenly, this thing he'd created started making all these demands on him and following him around," I said, trying not to look at Sharon. "And of course Victor assumed that he'd be in control of this being he'd created. But, and I believe this is the moral of the tale, once you start down the road of improving things, control tends to pass from the improver to the improvee. Which is exactly what happened to Victor and caused him untold heartache and grief."

I paused. De began to applaud. Others followed. Ryder whistled supportively.

"Wait," I said. "I'm not done. The thing that's really important is that that's exactly what's supposed to happen. If you help someone, they don't owe you and you don't *own* them. I mean, Victor and his monster were fictitious creatures. But real people aren't science fair projects. They like learn, change, grow, and move on."

I couldn't help it. I peeked at Sharon. She was sitting in the front row, decked out in this slammin' pale peach halter top with these striped cinnamon hip-huggers. Her golden hair was piled on her head and tied with fresh ribbons, and her sandaled feet were in the aisle, toenails pink and pedicured.

Again I fought to remember the girl who used to schlump into class late, wheezing apologies, all hunched up over her books. And again, faced with the glaring evidence of a truly chronic transformation, this strange feeling came over me. It wasn't pride. It was admiration.

It was like when I saw Sharon all feisty and full of herself at the Monster Bash. For one minute, in the ladies' room, I didn't see just this product of my brilliant makeover effort. I saw Sharon. And I realized for the first time, like really understood, that she was the one who'd changed. And that, just as she'd said, she used me to do it.

"The pleasure comes when you see the person you helped become the person they want to be," I concluded my report. "Which may so not be who you think they ought to be."

I gathered my notes together. De was staring at me, her brow furrowed. Amber's mouth was open, which was kind of business as usual. Murray had stopped polishing his trophy. Kimberly's hairbrush was motionless in her hand. It was like everyone was all, Duh, excuse me, what was that?

"Hello, that's it," I announced brightly. "That's what I learned."

Suddenly, Sharon scrambled to her Gucci-sandaled feet and began applauding enthusiastically. "Excellent presentation," she called out. "I was so moved. I totally felt Frankenstein's struggle and the creature's courage." She glanced over her shoulder and gave Raphael, who was saddle-soaping his leather jacket, this hard look. He leaped to his feet.

"Hey, yo!" Raph called. "You heard what Shar said. Let's hear it for a jammin' report."

"I second that emotion," Tai ardently announced, frantically clapping. Sean whistled and stomped. Amber raised her arms and waggled her fingers, which I chose to view as an expression of support rather than an attempt to dry her nail glue. And Ryder started tearing up his issue of *Fangoria* and going, "Powerful presentation, dude. Can't top that one, Mr. Hall. Why even bother, right?"

I did this adorable curtsy and headed back to my seat.

"I am so proud of you." De ran up the aisle and hugged me. "I'm like totally kvelling," she said. "When you started your report, I thought, Articulate, sensitive, we'll do an after-school celebration at Galleria. But when you summarized, I got all, Not even. It's got to be Rodeo Drive for the victory lap."

"Tomorrow, girlfriend. Lucas and I are catching a movie in Westwood tonight," I reminded her.

"This fly film just opened there." Murray joined us. *"Death Train from Cemetery Station,"* he said. "It's got everything, blood, guts, gore, psychos."

"Boys." De rolled her eyes dismissively. "They're like totally into Cuisinart flicks. You and Sean just love those dice 'em, slice 'em, puree and pulp 'em film classics. But Lucas is a senior, Murray. They're probably going to see something romantic."

"Romantic?" Murray's eyes bugged with disbelief. "Back me here, homes," he said to Sean. "Is there anything more romantic than chillin' in a dark venue, viewing ax-wielding maniacs with your main boo reduced to quivering desperation at your side?"

"Bliss," Sean confirmed.

The bell rang. We began gathering up our books. "They're not egregiously off base, De," I confided as Murray and Sean ambled off, shaking their heads. "Nothing tops the snuggle potential of a horror flick that drives you into the protective arms of your designated hottie."

Suddenly Olivia sidled up to me. "Cher," she said, toying nervously with her nose ring. The nostril in which it was embedded looked vaguely swollen and painfully raw. It was all I could do not to reach for my aloe vera gel.

"Can I speak with you privately?" she asked, blinking nervously. Flakes of dried mascara fluttered from her lashes, which I noticed were basically attractive and crying out for liberation. And then she uttered the fatal four words: "I need your help."

I practically swayed in her direction.

"I'm like totally desperate for a makeover and you're the only one who can—"

"No," a voice said gently. It took me a moment to realize that it was mine.

"I can't believe you said that." Olivia flung back her cruelly bleached hair with its tortured dark roots and glared at me.

Every fiber of my being longed to cry out to her, "Moisturize!" But I shook my head. Out of the corner of my eye, I saw Lucas waiting in the corridor, punching digits into his Motorola.

"Trust me, Olivia," I said, gathering up my books, my pink teddy bear backpack, my quilted Chanel shoulder bag, and my cellular—which of course was already ringing. "Neither can I!"

About the Author

H. B. Gilmour is the author of the bestselling noveli-
zations *Clueless* and *Pretty in Pink,* as well as
Clueless™: *Cher's Guide to . . . Whatever, Clueless*™:
Achieving Personal Perfection, Clueless™: *Friend or
Faux, Clueless*™: *Baldwin from Another Planet,
Clarissa Explains It All: Boys,* the well-reviewed
young-adult novel *Ask Me If I Care,* and more than
fifteen other books for adults and young people.